A Dead Man in Tangier

A DEAD MAN IN TANGIER

Michael Pearce

CARROLL & GRAF PUBLISHERS
NEW YORK

Carroll & Graf Publishers
An imprint of Avalon Publishing Group, Inc.
245 W. 17th Street, 11th Floor
New York, NY 10011-5300
www.carrollandgraf.com

AVALON
publishing group incorporated

First published in the UK by Constable,
an imprint of Constable & Robinson Ltd 2007

First Carroll & Graf edition 2007

ISBN-13: 978-0-78672-045-3
ISBN-10: 0-7867-2045-X

Printed and bound in the EU

Chapter One

'Pig-sticking. You know.'

Pig-sticking? Seymour didn't.

'As in India,' said the man from the Foreign Office helpfully.

What was India to do with Monsieur Bossu's death? Or pigs, for that matter?

'Really?' he said cautiously.

'Yes. Apparently there's a Tent Club. The only one outside India, they say.'

Still harping on about India. But the Superintendent, across in Whitechapel, had definitely said Africa. And what was all this about tents? If camping was going to be part of the investigation, Seymour was already losing enthusiasm.

'Is that so?' he said guardedly.

'Yes. There's an old boy who set it up, a local sheikh. Well, not just local. He's been Minister for War. He sets up the Tent and lays on the hospitality. And then they all come with their horses.'

'Really?'

'And spears.'

Spears! Jesus, what was this?

'And go for the pigs,' said the man from the Foreign Office happily. 'Not quite pigs, of course. Not in our sense. Boars, wild boars. And there's quite a difference, I can tell you! These will turn and come at you. With their tusks. They've got long, sharp tusks. And they really know about using them. Rip the horse's stomach open in a flash!'

'Rip the –?'

'And then set about the man.'

'It sounds –'

'– great fun,' said the man from the Foreign Office enthusiastically. 'Oh, it is! They come at you with such great speed, you see. And they're so mobile! They can double around like lightning. Much more quickly than a horse can. And then they come at you from a different angle. That's what gives them the edge.'

'Yes. Yes, I can see that. It would.'

'And that's what makes it such a good sport, of course.'

'Of course! Yes.'

Seymour hesitated.

'And that's what this chap, Bossu, was doing when –?'

'Yes.'

'But, look, if he was killed in action, so to speak, I don't see where I come in. Why send out a policeman? I mean, if a boar got him –'

'Oh, but it didn't.'

'No? Even so, if it was an accident –'

'Ah, but it wasn't.'

'No?'

'Someone,' said the man from the Foreign Office grimly, 'stuck him.'

Not exactly the kind of case that you usually got in the East End. But then, Seymour, these days, did not get the usual cases. With his flair for languages he was increasingly being sent abroad, much to the envy of his colleagues.

'Tangier,' said the sergeant dreamily. 'Isn't that where the oranges come from?'

'Palm trees,' muttered the constable behind the counter, going into a trance. 'Belly-dancers.'

That bit sounded all right, thought Seymour, tidying up

6

his papers. But what if the bellies were being ripped open by homicidal wild boars?

Less than a week later, however, there he was in a little steamer nudging its way along a brown, barren coast. Occasionally he caught glimpses of white houses huddled below unyielding cliffs. Gradually the cliff became green slopes and the rock retreated inland and became mountains veiled in mist. There was a mist on the sea, too, and for a while he lost sight of the land. Then, suddenly, the mists parted and there, floating uncertainly like a mirage, was a large bay fringed with palm trees, and inland, among the houses, a white-walled building. Its flat roofs rose gradually to culminate in a minaret whose coloured tiles flashed in the evening sun.

'The Kasbah,' said a voice beside him.

'I carry your baggage, sir?'

'No, I can manage.'

'I carry your baggage!' – insistently.

But other voices, also insistent.

'I carry . . .'

'I carry . . .'

'You carry,' said Seymour resignedly, pointing to the first man.

Not so simple.

Another man:

'Sir, sir, why bother with this man? I have donkey, big donkey, fine donkey –'

'I carry the donkey as well,' said the man already with his baggage. 'Bugger off!' he said to the donkey man.

An insistent hand (this belonged to a third, or perhaps it was fourth, fifth or sixth party):

'Why bother walk, sir? When you can ride? In my fine new carriage?'

It wouldn't have been new in Julius Caesar's time. Seymour took one look and shook his head.

But the man insisted.

'No, sir, look! Fine new carriage!'

He opened the cab door and a swarm of flies rose from the tattered upholstery.

'Thank you, no.'

His already chosen porter, who looked, actually, as if he could carry the cab as well, shouldered the cab man indignantly aside and set out determinedly.

'Just a minute, you don't know where –'

'But, yes, sir,' said the porter in injured tones. 'You are going to the Hotel Miramar.'

'Well, yes, I am,' said Seymour, surprised. 'But how did you –?'

'You are official, sir. All officials go to the Hotel Miramar.'

It wasn't far, which was just as well because Seymour was already bathed in sweat. He preferred it like this, however, as he wanted to give himself time to adjust.

They walked first beside the shore, past palm trees beneath which donkeys, their panniers filled with charcoal, waited patiently for customers while their masters squatted on their heels beside them gossiping with their neighbours, and then they turned up into the narrow, dark lanes of the old city, where he was suddenly hit by all sorts of exotic smells, and where girls with hennaed hands pottered past carrying water melons and small boys, some of them with startling auburn hair (Berber, wondered Seymour?) played in the dust.

They came to a square with a solitary tree, lit by a dim lantern, where merchants squatted beside mounds of brilliantly coloured spices. The air was full of incense and the fumes of frying oil.

There was the sound of a gunshot.

'It is to signify the end of the day's fast, sir. This is Ramadan.'

'It sounded as if it came from the mosque.'

'It did, sir.'

Around the edges of the square people were preparing

8

food. Bowls of soup were steaming, flat loaves of bread were neatly piled up, and in the pans over charcoal fires the hot food for the main meal was already simmering.

The porter led him off up a side-street between high white walls from the other side of which drifted the heavy perfumes of sweet-scented shrubs. They came to a white building with balconies fenced off by railings of iron fretwork, quite Spanish, Seymour thought: and why not? Spain was only a mile or two away across the straits.

'The Hotel Miramar, sir.'

He was shown to his room and walked out on to the balcony. Across the tops of the houses he could see the harbour with its thousands of lights and just off to his right he caught a glimpse of the Kasbah. From the European part of the city, further away, he could hear the castanets of the cabarets: Spanish, too.

But here it was quieter. When he listened he could hear the clicking of the crickets in the garden below him. The sounds of the square had disappeared almost entirely; except, occasionally, for the soft quavering of flutes.

He unpacked his things and went downstairs. In the foyer a young woman was sitting behind the desk. Later, he realized that this was unusual. Such jobs in the Arab world were normally filled by men.

She looked up from her writing and smiled.

'I am afraid we don't serve evening meals,' she said. 'But just around the corner there's a very good restaurant.'

When he stepped out of the hotel the air struck him as unbelievably warm. He shouldn't have put on his jacket. He went round the corner as she had suggested and found the restaurant.

After he had eaten, it was still early, and he walked down to the square. The post-fasting meals were still going on, the eaters sitting in small circles in the darkness around the charcoal fires. The merchants were still squatting beside their spices. The henna-handed little girls were still flitting about. Some of the shops were still open and in the dim light of their oil lamps he could see the shopkeepers weighing out raisins and spreading bales of cloth for the women to fondle.

By the time he had completed his circuit of the square the moon had come out and was lighting up the roofs of the houses. The minaret he had noticed earlier had lost its colours and become a mysterious silver, and as he turned back up the road towards the hotel he found that the sand underfoot, where the moon fell upon it, had changed to silver too.

In the street outside the hotel it was as bright as day. A knot of men suddenly burst into it. The knot became two groups which surged around each other. There were shouts and cries and the flash of knives in the moonlight.

One of the men fell and another man stooped over him. Seymour saw the knife and shouted. The man looked up, startled. The man beneath rolled away.

Seymour shouted again and began to run towards them. The knot wavered and then broke up and in a moment there was only the man lying there.

Seymour bent over him. There was something wet and sticky on the front of his shirt and he was holding his arm across his chest. Seymour moved it away to see the extent of the damage and the man gave a little moan.

He became aware that someone was standing beside him and spun round. The man stepped back and held up his hand apologetically.

'Pardon!' he said.

The man on the ground looked up.

'Where the hell have you been?' he said, in French.

The other man knelt down beside him.

'Are you all right?'

'No, I'm bloody not!'

'Can you stand?'

The man grunted and put out a hand. His friend took it and helped him up. The wounded man gave a little gasp.

Then he put an arm round his friend's shoulders and stood for a moment, swaying.

A door opened and light fell down the hotel's steps.

A woman's voice said:

'I will not have this! Not in front of the hotel!'

'Sorry, Chantale!' said the wounded man humbly.

'It started further up the road,' explained his friend. 'I don't know how it came to drift down.'

'See it doesn't happen again!'

She went back inside. It was the receptionist.

The wounded man said something to his friend and the two wobbled across to Seymour. They stopped in front of him and the wounded man detached his arm from his friend's shoulders and made a little formal bow.

'To you, Monsieur, I owe thanks.'

'It was nothing.'

'Ah, but it was something. I shall not forget.'

They all three shook hands formally in the French way, and then the two men set off up the road, the one supporting the other.

The receptionist was back behind her desk, head down. She gave Seymour a little flicker of acknowledgement but barely looked up from her writing. Seymour started off up the stairs.

A porter was just coming down. He glanced at Seymour and then said something to the receptionist. This time she stopped her writing and looked up.

'There is blood on your coat,' she said, matter-of-factly. 'Take it off and I will have it cleaned for you. It will be ready for you in the morning.'

The affair was otherwise dismissed. So this is how it is, thought Seymour, in Tangier?

When he came down the next morning she was there at her desk, writing again. She jumped up when she saw him.

'I am afraid you have caught us out,' she said. 'I did not expect to see you so early. I had to send your coat out and it's not back yet. My people here couldn't quite get the blood all off but there's a good little tailor in the square who is used to this sort of thing.'

Used to this sort of thing? Blood on your coat?

'It will be ready, I promise you. I can send someone down immediately. But . . .' She hesitated. 'Were you thinking of wearing it? Here in Tangier?'

'Why not?'

'You'll be too hot. People don't usually bother with jackets in Tangier.'

'I have to see the Consul.'

'He won't be wearing one, either,' she said drily. 'What you could do is get Ali to make you up something in lightweight suiting. He would do it very nicely and you would have it by this evening. And it wouldn't cost you much. Two pounds.'

'Two pounds?'

'Yes. He might suggest more, but just say you're a friend of Chantale.'

'Thanks. I'll think about it.'

It didn't take long. When he stepped outside, the heat hit him like a hammer.

'Where did you say this tailor was?'

'In the square. His name is Ali. He's very good. And you can pick up the jacket at the same time.'

It was the tailor he had noticed the previous evening. When Seymour went in he was sitting on the counter, sewing. All the shopkeepers sat on their counters. The things they sold were stacked on shelves around the walls.

'Ali?'

'Monsieur?'

'I think you've been cleaning a jacket for me.'

'Ah, yes.'

He climbed down off the counter and reached up behind a curtain.

'Thank you.'

The coat was spotless.

The tailor weighed it in his hands. 'Good cloth,' he said.

'But a bit heavy for here, perhaps. I was wondering if you could make up something for me?'

'I certainly could. Would you like to look at my materials? This one, for instance. Just right for you.'

'How much?'

'Six pounds.'

'Chantale said you would do it for two.'

'Ah, Chantale? Well, that's a bit different. Yes, well,' – regretfully – 'I suppose I *could* do it for two.'

He held the cloth up against Seymour.

'That girl,' he muttered to himself, 'will be the ruin of me.'

Then he brightened.

'But also, perhaps, the making of me!'

A man came into the shop, saw Seymour and slipped out again.

The tailor asked Seymour to put on a dummy jacket and then began to mark it with chalk.

The man came back, bringing a friend with him.

'Hello, Ali!'

'Idris! And Mustapha, too.'

They seemed familiar. He suddenly realized. They were the ones he'd met the previous night.

Seymour's jacket was lying on the counter. The wounded man came across and touched it.

'That his jacket?'

'Yes. I've just been cleaning it –'

'It's on me.'

'Why this sudden generosity, Mustapha?'

'It's my blood.'

'Oh!' The tailor tut-tutted.

'That business last night?'

'Yes.'

The tailor shook his head.

'You ought to keep out of things like that,' he said to Seymour.

13

'I'll try not to make it a habit.'

'No, but really . . . You're a stranger here?'

Idris broke in.

'That's just what I said to Mustapha. He's a stranger here, I said. And doesn't know any better.'

'Just as well he didn't know any better,' growled Mustapha.

'Yes, I know, but, all the same, he ought to keep out of it.'

'Don't worry,' said Seymour, 'I have every intention of doing that.'

'Did you know,' asked Ali, 'that he's a friend of Chantale?'

'What? Oh, my God!' said Idris. 'She's not best pleased with us just at the moment.'

'Maybe you ought to keep out of things yourself for a bit, too,' suggested Ali.

'That's just what I said to Mustapha this morning!' said Idris.

'Yes, but how can I keep out of things and let a friend of mine wander round like an innocent?' asked Mustapha.

'Look, I know he's your friend now. He's a friend of mine, too. But –'

'Everyone in the bilad knows he's my friend. Or soon will.'

'I know, I know. But –'

'It would look *bad*,' said Mustapha, 'if something happened to him. A friend of mine and I let something bad happen to him! What would people say! I could never show my face again.'

'Well, I know. I couldn't, either. A friend of yours is a friend of mine. It would look bad.'

'I could never hold up my head in public again.'

'Well, I know. But –' He turned to Seymour. 'Look, how long are you likely to be in Tangier for?'

'I don't know. Perhaps three weeks. But –'

'We *could* look after him,' said Idris tentatively. 'For that long. Three weeks is nothing.'

14

'Nothing!' agreed Mustapha, as if a weight had been lifted from his shoulders. 'Easy!'

'Look, thank you very much but I don't really need anyone to look after me –'

The two men caught each other's eye and nodded.

'Right, that's it,' said Idris. 'Where are you going today, then?'

'To the British Consul's. But –'

'The *British* Consul?' said Mustapha significantly.

'That's right. But –'

'Just a minute,' said Idris, 'wasn't that bloke who got taken out something to do with him? A Frenchman. What was his name?'

'Bossu!' said Ali. 'He used to come to my shop. Here.'

'Bossu!' said Idris.

'That's right.'

'Then you certainly do need our protection,' said Mustapha, turning to Seymour.

When Seymour set out for the British Consulate a little later, his two new friends, despite everything he could do, swaggered along behind him.

'So you're Seymour?' said the Consul unenthusiastically.

'That's right.'

'From Scotland Yard. Well, you'll find things a bit different here.'

'I don't know,' said Seymour. 'I worked in the East End.'

'Where's that?'

Seymour looked at him to see if he was joking; then decided to make allowance for him being in the Foreign Office.

'The East End of London. It's a rough area. There are a lot of immigrants. Italians, Greeks, Jews, Poles – Central Europeans of all kind.'

'It's a bit of a mixture here, too. But not immigrants. They belong here. And they all think they own the place.'

'Who does it belong to?'

'Aye, that's the problem. What languages do you speak?'

'French, German, Italian – most of the European ones. And some Arabic.'

'Just because they're Moroccan, that doesn't mean that they speak Arabic. A lot of them speak Berber. But French will be useful. They're the ones who currently think they own the place.'

'Well, don't they?'

'They've just established a Protectorate here. That doesn't mean to say that they own the place. As I think they'll very shortly find. But, yes, they're the ones we currently have to deal with.'

'And Monsieur Bossu was the man you had to deal with most?'

'No. He was there to deal with *me*.'

He looked out of the window.

'What are those two hooligans doing there?'

Mustapha and Idris were squatting on the verandah outside.

'They're . . . acquaintances of mine.'

'They're drug dealers!'

'Very probably.'

The Consul looked at him hard.

'You're not –?'

'No.' He told the Consul how he had come to meet them. 'What sort of drugs do they deal in?'

'Kif. It's like marijuana. Everyone takes kif around here. It's so normal that nobody thinks about it. But it's profitable to people to deal in it.' He looked out of the window again. 'Although not, I would think, for those two.'

He came back and sat down.

'Tell me about Bossu,' said Seymour.

'He was clerk to a committee I'm Chairman of. The committee was set up following a complex series of international negotiations which led first to France's declaration of a Protectorate over Morocco – that was in March – and then to an agreement between France and Spain broadly to the effect that Spain would keep out of it in return for a

16

Spanish-owned zone along the coast. The status of Tangier and the land around it, which is of interest to a lot of countries, including ourselves, was left out of it but there was broad agreement that it should be given a special character, roughly, that it should become a free city supervised by a committee which includes representatives of all the Great Powers. The working details were left to this committee: of which I am Chairman.'

'And Bossu was clerk?'

'Yes.'

'Put in by France to see that the committee did not stray too far from France's interests?'

'Not quite. Or, rather, not just. There are other interests as well, commercial ones, which are very strong in Tangier. Most are French but not all. Bossu was there to keep them happy as well – their interests may well be different from those of the French Government and through their own contacts they have a strong voice in Paris. Bossu, you could say, was a Tangierian, and that's not quite the same as a Frenchman, and not at all the same as a Moroccan.'

'And these conflicting interests may have had something to do with his death?'

'That is what I want you to find out.'

'So tell me about the pig-sticking. Which was where, I gather, he met his end.'

'You know about pig-stickings? They're a bit like an English hunt. Or so they tell me – I've never been to one myself,' he said, with the disdain of a Scot for his savage English neighbours.

'They meet on horses . . .?'

'Aye. With lances, to stick the pigs.'

'The pigs . . .?'

'Are wild. You find them in the scrub outside Tangier. There's woodland nearby where they can feed. Well, the huntsmen meet at a special place. A local worthy puts up a tent and they have a splendid feast afterwards, which is half the point of the exercise. Some pigs are rounded up and set loose and then off they go.

'Well, Bossu was among the huntsmen – it's a popular sport among the settlers – and was seen chasing after a boar which had darted off at a tangent into the bushes. Bossu had followed him, apparently alone – and it was only some time later that they found him lying face down in the sand with a lance stuck between his shoulders.'

'And no one saw –?'

'That's what they claim.'

'But surely someone – I mean, there were clearly a lot of people around.'

'Aye, but the hunt was moving on. Everyone was watching the pigs, and the pigs were running hard, and you didn't want to lose sight of them –'

'Weren't there people behind, on foot?'

'Oh, aye; half Morocco.'

'Then –?'

'They were watching the pigs, too.'

'But surely someone must have seen something. He was on a horse, wasn't he? High up. Above the scrub. How high is the scrub there?'

'Five feet, six feet.'

'Then –'

'No one saw anything. All two hundred of them rushed past. They say. To be fair, there were probably lots of other exciting things going on.'

'Okay. So no one saw anything and the hunt moved on?'

'And eventually came to a stop several miles away. The stickers then made their way slowly back to the Tent and it was only quite some time later that someone noticed that Bossu wasn't there. And some time after that when someone was sent back to see if he had fallen.'

'Who was sent back?'

'The Sheikh sent two of his men.'

'The Sheikh?'

'Sheikh Musa. The one who organizes the feast. A fine

18

old boy. Used to be Minister of War. He walked out in disgust when the Sultan signed the treaty establishing the French Protectorate.'

'And the two men found the body?'

'Lying face down. With a lance stuck between his shoulders. It was still there, apparently. Standing straight up, the men said. Like a flagpole.'

He smiled wryly.

'A good stick, I think pig-stickers would say.'

Chapter Two

'I suppose,' said the Consul, after they had taken tea, 'that you would like to visit the scene of the crime? Isn't that what you fellows usually do?'

Seymour allowed that it was: and they took one of the little fly-blown cabs waiting beneath the palm trees and headed out of town. Their way took them first along a wide boulevard fringed with vivid clumps of bougain-villea and then, leaving behind them the white, crowded streets of the Old City, they entered a completely different area. Rising up a slope to their right were rows of low European-style villas, each in a patch of green with bright bursts of oleander and bougainvillea.

'The European quarter,' said Macfarlane. 'Bossu had a house here, where he lived with Mrs Bossu. And an apartment in town where he lived with someone who wasn't Mrs Bossu.'

Beyond the villas were cultivated fields and small farms, which gave way to stony desert scattered with thin, thorny scrub; and then, rising incongruously out of the scrub, was a large black and white marquee which reminded Seymour of an English County Show which he had once mistakenly visited.

'The Tent,' said Macfarlane, with pride.

In front of the marquee were wagons and blue-gowned figures unloading barrels, which they were taking inside. As each barrel was carried through the entrance it was ticked off on a list by a harassed-looking Frenchman.

'Monsieur L'Espinasse,' said Macfarlane. 'Our Secretary.'

He came across to greet them.

'Monsieur L'Espinasse, Monsieur Seymour.' Macfarlane spoke in French. 'Seymour has just arrived from England. He's come to look into the Bossu business.'

A shade of discomfort crossed the Secretary's face.

'Ah, Bossu!' He looked at Macfarlane. 'Some people have suggested we ought to cancel,' he said. 'As a mark of respect. But others have said that they didn't feel much respect for Bossu and that it ought to go ahead.'

'You can't cancel for every little thing,' said the Consul.

'My thought exactly,' said the Secretary, relieved. 'Are you coming tomorrow?' he said to Seymour. 'You'd be very welcome. Come as my guest.'

'There's a pig-sticking tomorrow?'

'Yes. Most Saturdays during the season.'

'I would very much like to.'

Out of the corner of his eye Seymour saw Idris and Mustapha detach themselves from the rear of the cab, where they had been riding on the axle.

'De Grassac here?' asked Macfarlane.

'Out the back,' said the Secretary.

They went round to the back of the marquee, where they found a group of men who had just been practising. Their lances were stuck in the ground beside their horses, which were still breathing heavily. The men were in military overalls and seemed to be soldiers. Instead of a cap or a helmet they wore a kind of Bedouin headdress.

'Ah, de Grassac! Captain de Grassac,' he said to Seymour, 'was the man who was sent out to see to the body when word came in.'

De Grassac nodded. He was a tall, fiercely moustached man with a deeply suntanned, open face and sharp blue eyes.

'This is Monsieur Seymour. He's come out to look into this Bossu business. I wonder if you would mind showing him the spot?'

'Not at all,' said de Grassac. 'Shall we go now?'

He hesitated.

'Do you ride? No? Then you'd better come up behind me.'

As they rode away Seymour saw Idris and Mustapha standing nearby and looking, for the moment, distinctly perplexed.

De Grassac threaded his way confidently through the thorn. At first the sand was heavily scuffed up where the main hunt had passed, but then he turned away and went off through patches of thick scrub where they soon lost sight of the main track.

And where, presumably, the people on the main track would have lost sight of them. Seymour began to understand how it was that no one appeared to have seen Bossu.

The ground rose and fell in little hillocks and valleys and in the hollows, although the scrub was usually only shoulder height, it would be easy to lose sight of a man, even a horseman.

De Grassac came to a stop and jumped down. For a moment he walked his horse round scrutinizing the ground. Then he pointed. Looking closely, Seymour fancied that the sand was slightly discoloured.

He slid unskilfully from the horse's back.

There ought to be some signs. If he had been a Boy Scout perhaps he would have detected them. But Seymour was not a Boy Scout and so far in his career in the East End of London he had not been called on to display any of those skills at tracking and reading spoor that that madman, Baden Powell, who still regularly occupied the newspapers, seemed so keen on. Today, however, he could have done with them.

'How was he lying?'

The Captain spread his arms.

'Face down?'

De Grassac nodded.

'And with the lance in his back,' he said.

22

'Pinning him?'

'It had gone right through and the point was embedded in the ground. I had difficulty in pulling it out. I had to pull it out so that they could move him.'

'That suggests considerable force.'

De Grassac nodded.

'It's the way you're taught to stick,' he said. 'Thrust hard and thrust down.'

'You think he was killed by someone in the hunt?'

'It was a huntsman's lance, wasn't it?'

Seymour tried to visualize it. It was not the kind of thing that he was used to visualizing.

'You are assuming, then, that he was already lying on the ground when he was stabbed?'

'It's not easy to stick someone on a horse,' said de Grassac. 'I know. I've tried it.'

'As a soldier?'

'As a soldier, yes. We sometimes use lances against the tribesmen.'

'But it's not easy?'

'The tribesmen are usually on foot. But I have tried it against horsemen. No, it's not easy. The target is moving all the time. So are the pigs, of course. But the thing is, with a pig you can strike down. If a man's on a horse, you have to strike parallel with the ground and get your lance to steady. And the ground's going up and down, and the horse in front is, too. And, besides, there's the question of force. It's difficult to strike hard enough if you're striking forward. Whereas when you're striking down –'

'So you think he was already on the ground?'

'Yes.'

'He must have fallen, then.'

De Grassac spread his hands.

'Something in the bushes,' he said. 'A snake, perhaps.'

'Or a man?'

'Or a man.'

'You're the expert on this. Might he have been stabbed by a man on the ground?'

'No,' said de Grassac shortly.

If he had fallen there ought to be some signs of this. A Boy Scout would have picked them out. Seymour, however, could see nothing at all.

This kind of thing was not for him. He felt like a fish out of water. Sand, scrub, space . . . He was used to the tight little confines of built-up, urban London. Out here, with the huge sky, sand going on for ever, not a building or a person in sight, nor a sound, only the wind oozing thin through the thorn bushes, he was entirely out of his natural element.

'What happened to the lance?' he asked.

'I've got it,' said de Grassac, surprisingly.

'You've got it?'

'Lances cost money. You don't leave them lying around. You do not, perhaps, understand how things are here, Monsieur. You have to watch over things or else they will be taken. Anything. They would have stripped the body. In fact, I was surprised when I got here to find that they hadn't done that already. Of course, Musa had sent back two of his men as soon as it became clear that Bossu hadn't come in, and after that one of them had always stayed with the body. But that all took time, and, as I say, I was surprised that the body had not already been stripped. This is not England, Monsieur.'

No, thought Seymour, it certainly was not.

Back at the Tent the Secretary was talking to a short, wiry Moroccan dressed in a kind of cavalry tunic and riding breeches and boots. He spotted Seymour and waved to him to join them.

'Monsieur Seymour, may I present you to our patron? Sheikh Musa. Monsieur Seymour,' he explained to the Sheikh, 'has come out from London to investigate Bossu's death.'

'From London? An Englishman?'

They shook hands.

24

'An Englishman to investigate a Frenchman's death? Now why is that?'

Seymour started to explain about the international committee but Musa cut him short.

'I know about the committee,' he said. 'You know what they say about it? That everything has already been decided and that it's just there to dress things up.'

He spoke perfect French.

'I don't know anything about that,' said Seymour. 'I am concerned only with Bossu's death.'

'Ah, but they say that this *is* to do with Bossu's death.'

'Why do they say that?'

'Bossu was the clerk. Some say he was put there to fix it. So that the French could get what they want.'

'Now, Sheikh Musa,' began the Secretary, 'you're being provocative –'

'But that he didn't fix it. And so they decided to get rid of him.'

'Sheikh Musa –'

'But I don't believe that. They could have got rid of him without killing him. And, anyway, Bossu would always have done what he was told. So it must be something else. Others say that he was killed for just the opposite reason. So that the French – in the French Government, that is, there are different sorts of French out here – *shouldn't* get what they wanted.'

'Who would take that view?'

'The settlers. They've been having things their way for a long time. And they'd like that to continue.'

'Sheikh Musa, I really must protest. The settlers – the business community as a whole – want only what is best for the country.'

'Yes,' said Sheikh Musa, eyes glinting wickedly, 'but which country?'

The Consul joined them at that point.

'Are you having a go at him, Musa?' he asked.

25

'It's the only thing I can do now,' growled the Sheikh. 'Now that there are French soldiers all over the place.'

'Now, come on, Musa,' said the Consul, 'you know you've got to go along with it. Now that the Sultan has signed the agreement.'

'It should never have been signed!'

'Maybe. But it *has* been signed and now we've got to move on.'

'The Sultan should go!'

'And probably will,' said the Consul cheerfully. 'But, then, who will replace him?'

'Some French ass-licker,' growled Musa.

'It's no good, Musa. You'll have to hang up your sword. And stick to your lance in future. Work it off on the pigs.'

'I could do that,' said Sheikh Musa, brightening. He turned to Seymour.

'We're having a sticking tomorrow,' he said. 'Would you like to come?'

'Monsieur L'Espinasse has already invited me. Thank you, I would. Yes. Very much.'

'Have you a horse? No? No, of course you wouldn't have. Never mind, I'll lend you one. Two, if you like! I've got lots of horses.'

'Well, that's very kind of you, but –'

'The English are good at hunting.'

'Actually, I –'

'That's where I got the idea from, you know,' Musa said to the Secretary. 'From the English. In India. I went over there with a delegation. The British wanted to show us their army. Impress us. At the time they had designs on Morocco themselves but then, of course, they came to an agreement with the French whereby they would let France have Morocco if the French would let them have Egypt. But at the time I went they were still interested in Morocco and they wanted to soften us up. So they invited us over to India to see their army. Well, I wasn't too impressed by the army. But the pig-sticking! That really was something!'

The marquee was filling up. All sorts of people had drifted in, soldiers, officials of various kinds, often in uniforms, too, as well as what seemed to Seymour ordinary business-men in suits, drawn, Seymour suspected from the beeline they made for the bar, chiefly by the promise of a free drink. Or maybe, since there were so many Frenchmen here, it was just aperitif time.

Among the newcomers, he was slightly surprised to see, was the receptionist from his hotel, as in command of the situation as always, moving round from one group to another, recognized, apparently by everybody, and chatting to everyone. She noticed Seymour and came across to him.

'Hello!' she said. 'Have you had a fruitful morning?'

'Interesting, certainly. I don't know about fruitful.'

'And have you found out anything?'

'Found out anything?'

'About Bossu.'

'You know what I'm here for, then?'

'Of course. In Tangier everyone knows everything. And I have a particular interest in Bossu.'

Macfarlane suddenly appeared beside them.

'Be careful, Seymour!' he warned. 'Anything you say could be in the newspaper.'

'Only if it's scandalous,' said the receptionist. 'And Mon-sieur Seymour has hardly been here long enough to learn about our scandals. Or, indeed, contribute to them.'

'I'll do my best,' promised Seymour.

'What's the latest, Chantale?' asked Macfarlane.

'It's all very quiet. Juliette is being her usual self but people feel it's a bit indecent so soon.'

'Mademoiselle is a journalist as well as a receptionist?' asked Seymour.

'Chantale is a gossip columnist,' said Macfarlane. 'And

what better place for a gossip columnist than the reception desk of an important hotel?'

'I am not *just* a gossip columnist,' said Chantale. 'I am an investigative journalist too.'

'If I were you,' said Macfarlane. 'I'd stick to the gossip. There's more money in it.'

'Ah, yes,' said Chantale, 'but less excitement.'

A short, plump man with enormous waxed moustaches came up to Seymour and threw his arms around him.

'*Cher collègue!*' he cried.

'*Collègue!*' cried Seymour, returning the embrace but a little surprised.

The little man stepped back, drew himself together and bowed.

'Renaud,' he said. 'Chief of Police.'

'Ah! Seymour –'

'I know, I know. Monsieur Macfarlane has told me. Welcome to Tangier, Monsieur. An aperitif, to welcome your arrival!'

He piloted Seymour over to a corner where the soldiers were standing around a small table on which there were several bottles of wine.

'A friend!' he cried. 'From England.'

'From England? Welcome, Monsieur!'

Someone handed him a glass.

'Monsieur Seymour. From Scotland Yard,' said Renaud proudly.

'Scotland . . .?'

'*Yard,*' said the Chief of Police with emphasis. 'It is the quarters of the English police.'

'Headquarters?'

The soldiers were impressed.

But then, recovering, not too impressed.

'But why, Monsieur, have you come out to this dump?'

'He is investigating the death of Bossu.'

'Bossu? Bossu!' – incredulously. 'But why?'

'Why, indeed? said Seymour swiftly. 'When the investigation is already in the capable hands of Monsieur
Renaud!'

'Ah, Monsieur . . .' said Renaud, self-deprecatingly.

'But these things are decided higher up,' said Seymour,
'and not always for reasons which are comprehensible.'

'You can say that again!'

There were general nods.

'Yes, but – Bossu, though!'

One of the officers laid his finger along his nose.

'It's politics.'

'Ah, politics.'

Shrugs all round.

'Even so – Bossu! Must have been more important than
I thought.'

'How have you been getting on, Renaud?'

'With the investigation? Oh, well. Well.'

'Found out anything yet?' said someone maliciously.

'My inquiries are proceeding,' said the Chief of Police
loftily.

'But are they getting anywhere?'

Renaud ignored this.

'I am putting up posters,' he said.

'That really should make a difference!'

'Offering a reward. A big one.'

'Who's paying for it?' asked someone sceptically.

'The community generally. Business leaders.'

'They would,' someone muttered.

'And settlers. I've had offers from the farmers.'

'Phew! He must be important, if they're willing to part
with a few of *their* francs.'

'Monsieur Bossu was a deeply respected member of the
business community of Tangier,' Renaud said, turning to
Seymour. 'And of Tangier.'

'Fiddles everywhere,' muttered someone.

'You may scoff,' said the Chief of Police, turning on
him, 'but when you've been in the country as long as
I have –'

There was a general jeer. Evidently it was a favourite phrase of his.

'How is Juliette, Renaud?' asked someone, when it had died down.

'She's all right. In a state of shock, of course. But getting over it.'

'I'll bet. Getting over it pretty quickly, I expect.'

'A poor woman!' said Renaud reprovingly. 'Alone. In a foreign country.'

'Well, I don't expect she'll be alone for long,' said someone. 'Going over to comfort her, are you, Renaud?'

'I *was* thinking of going over there, as a matter of fact.'

'Give her my love!'

'And mine!'

'And mine!'

'This is Madame Bossu you're talking about?' asked Seymour.

'That's right.'

'I would like to meet her.'

'Who wouldn't?'

The Consul was talking to two grey-haired men. He beckoned Seymour over.

'You might like to have a word with Monsieur Meunier,' he said. 'He's our doctor. He saw Bossu when he was brought in.'

'Millet's a doctor, too,' said Monsieur Meunier, 'and a more important one.'

'Ah, no!' protested the other man, laughing.

'He sees to the horses. I only see to the men. Horses are more important. They cost more.'

'Are there many injuries?' asked Seymour.

'Many, but minor. Cuts, bruises. The occasional collar bone. Dislocated shoulders.'

'I've just been over there,' said Seymour. 'I'm not surprised that people come off.'

'They come off less than you might think,' said Millet.

'Most of them are pretty experienced. And the horses are experienced too.'

'Was Bossu experienced?' asked Seymour.

'Bossu experienced?' Meunier frowned. 'Well, was he?' he said, turning to Millet.

'He rode a lot. He came over here regularly when the season was on.'

'Ah, but that was only to impress Monique.'

'Monique?'

'His *petite amie*. Little friend. Little *feminine* friend. I didn't get the feeling, though, that he enjoyed *la chasse* very much.'

'He always pulled out early.'

'I think that may have been why he went after that pig. So early, I mean. There was no need to. The main hunt was on ahead. But I think he suddenly saw a chance to stick a pig and then stop.'

'And get back to the Tent for a drink,' said Meunier.

'And to Monique.'

'Well, that wasn't stupid!' They both laughed.

'So he went off after the pig?' said Seymour.

'Yes. It darted off at a tangent and he went after it.'

'What happened after that? Did anyone see?'

'No, they were all rushing on. But they said they'd seen him making off to the left.'

'The ground is very uneven there,' said Seymour. 'Do you think he could have come off?'

'He could, I suppose. He wasn't that good a horseman.'

'You saw him when he was brought in, I gather: was there anything that might suggest a fall?'

'Cuts, bruising, you mean? Well, yes. But then he would have had to have fallen at some point, wouldn't he? If he was on a horse.'

'Well, that's the question, actually. Was he on a horse when he was stabbed? De Grassac thinks he was on the ground. The lance, you see, was pinning him.'

'It passed right through,' said Meunier. 'There were entry and exit wounds.'

31

'Monsieur Millet, I turn to you. The horse. You see to any horses which have been injured, if I remember. I wondered if you had seen Monsieur Bossu's horse when it was brought in? It *was* brought in, I presume?'

'Oh, yes. Some time later. One of Musa's men recognized it.'

'Did you get a chance to take a look at it?'

'Yes.'

'And were there any signs of injury?'

'Not really. No indication of a hobble, which there might have been if it had put a foot wrong, for instance. Easy to on that ground and that might have brought Bossu off. But there was no suggestion of that. Just –'

'Just!'

'Prickles. Thorns. Well, there are always plenty of those, of course, especially after they've been going through this kind of scrub. But I remember noticing that there were an unusual quantity of thorns in Bossu's horse. Now, of course, if it had panicked and been crashing around in the bushes that would explain it. But I remember noticing that most of them were in the horse's flanks, which made me think that it might have backed into a thorn bush, if, say, it had been startled by something in front of it . . . Well, that's all I can offer, I'm afraid.'

Monsieur Meunier had been toying with his glass.

'Did you say that de Grassac thought Bossu had been stabbed while he was lying on the ground?'

'Yes.'

'Well, that's not very nice, is it? I mean, I never had much time for Bossu, but that makes it sound as if he was stuck like a pig.'

'That's not the only thing,' said Millet. 'It makes it sound as it he was stuck by, well, one of *us*.'

It was agreed that Renaud would take Seymour with him. Seymour had not wanted to cramp his style, but Renaud seemed quite happy with the arrangement.

'Juliette will be glad to see you,' he assured him. 'It will satisfy her that everything that can be done is being done.'

They set off in one of the soiled, tatty cabs, which Seymour had assumed were mainly used for the transporting of flies. There were several waiting optimistically outside the marquee. Optimistically, but not urgently. They seemed relaxed about time in Tangier.

'It will wait for us while we're talking to Juliette,' the Chief of Police said. 'Or perhaps' – having second thoughts – 'for you if Juliette wants me to stay.'

Seymour thought that quite likely.

The cab took them back the way they had come and then turned up the slope to the rows of bougainvillea villas. It came to a stop outside one of the larger ones, where a woman was on the verandah watering some plants.

'Constant!'

'Juliette!'

'And you have brought a friend with you!'

'Monsieur Seymour. From London. He has come out here –'

'To assist Monsieur Renaud,' said Seymour swiftly.

'– in the matter of Bossu.'

'Ah!'

Madame Bossu stepped off the verandah into the sunlight and he saw at once what the officers had meant. If that was your type. Blonde, peaches-and-cream complexion, full, pouting lips.

'Then I wish you every success, Monsieur, in all your ventures here.'

Spoken in a low, husky voice and giving a hint, surely, that the ventures might not be restricted to *l'affaire Bossu*.

'I am so sorry, Madame, to hear about your misfortune.'

'I loved him,' she said tragically. 'And now he is gone. And I am left desolate.'

'But not alone, Juliette,' said Monsieur Renaud.

'Not alone,' agreed Juliette, permitting herself a tender smile, 'when I have friends like you.'

33

'At your service,' said Renaud fervently. 'Always!'

'Constant is a great support to me,' she said to Seymour, 'and at a time like this one needs support. There are so many things to sort out. Wills, banks –'

'Insurance,' murmured the Chief of Police.

'And how is the insurance coming along?'

'We're getting there. It takes time. All these things are a little more complicated than you think.'

'Everything Bossu did was complicated,' sighed Madame Bossu.

'He had so many interests! The business ones especially will take some time to sort out.'

'I know. And all over the country, too! Casablanca, Marrakesh. Fez, Rabat –'

'And complicated! You wouldn't believe how complicated they are, Juliette.'

'But you will sort them out,' said Madame Bossu confidently. 'I know I can rely on you, Constant. Above all other men.'

'You can, Juliette, you can. But it all takes time. You must be patient, Juliette. And keep your spirits up. You are too much alone. You need company, Juliette, someone to take you out of yourself.'

'I have good, kind friends,' said Juliette, sighing.

'You have, Juliette. But they may not be enough. There will be times when you are alone at night –'

'I hope you are not going to suggest anything improper, Constant!'

'At a time like this? Oh, Juliette, how could you think that! I was thinking of you. Alone in that big house. Thinking sad thoughts. You need someone there when your friends are not there. Someone to stay with you and cheer you up –'

'Constant, you *are* being improper!'

'Not at all! I protest, not at all! I was thinking' – casting around – 'of a woman.'

34

'A woman!' said Juliette coldly.

'As a companion for you. At this distressing time.'

'I hope you were not thinking of Monique.'

'The last person I would think of!'

'That bitch!'

'Come, now, Juliette. Be generous. She shares your loss.'

'She wants to share the money. He's not left her anything, has he? That apartment —'

'It does belong to her, Juliette. It is registered in her name.'

'But it belongs to me! It was bought with Bossu's money. My money!'

'But it's in her name, Juliette. That's the problem.'

'Well, you'll just have to do something about it. Get it off her. You're looking after my interests, Constant. *My* interests. Not hers. Unless — Oh, Constant! You're not betraying me with that bitch, are you? Oh, Constant! How could you!'

'I assure you, I assure you —'

'Monsieur Seymour, you are not going to stand by and see a poor woman robbed?'

She turned towards him her beautiful tear-stained face.

'Assuredly not, Madame!' said Seymour fervently, carried away, for the moment.

'Juliette —' began Renaud wretchedly.

'You cannot imagine, Monsieur,' she said, looking up at Seymour with blue, tragic eyes, 'what it is for a woman to lose her husband in such a way. Murdered! Killed by those fanatics!'

'I'm sorry?'

'*Les nègres*. The blacks. They hate us, you know. And they hated him. Even though he had lived in the country for all that time. Thirty years! He gave his life to this damned country. And see how they repay him!'

'But, Juliette, we do not know —'

'Of course we do! Who else could it have been? A spear,

35

in the bushes? From behind? That is how they fight. And how they kill!'

Renaud, discomfited, did not, after all, stay behind and he and Seymour drove into Tangier together. As they reached the bottom of the slope and slowed down to turn into Tangier, Seymour felt the carriage tip suddenly at the rear and guessed that they had been joined.

Chapter Three

The city, when they got there, was oddly still. The streets were empty. The peanut sellers, sticky-sweet sellers and dirty postcard sellers with whom they had previously been crowded had all vanished. The beggars, who had been at least as numerous, had retired into the shade. The shops were not exactly closed – their fronts remained open to the world – but no one was in them. It was, he suddenly realized, the hour of siesta.

Renaud shook hands and departed and Seymour, with nothing to do until five o'clock, when he was seeing Macfarlane, went back to his hotel.

That, too, was deserted. He had half hoped to see the receptionist again and was slightly disappointed when he didn't. She was still probably doubling up as a journalist at the Tent.

The coolness of the hotel, though, was welcome after the heat outside and he climbed up the marble stairs to his room and lay on the bed. He knew he wouldn't be able to sleep – he never could during the day – but he felt a need to sort out the jumble of impressions which had crowded in on him in the short forty-eight hours that he had been in Tangier: the variety of peoples – Arab, Berber, French, Jewish, Negroes (from the Sudan? or West Africa?); the exotic, besieging smells of spices and sand and fresh leather and sandalwood – even the bales of cloth in the tailor's shop had smelt differently from the way they would have done in England; the different perfumes of the women, light, intoxicating in the case of the Frenchwomen, heavy, sensuous in the case of the Moroccans; the bright colours of the long gowns, pink and salmon and hectic green and blue, alongside the blackness of the veiled women, the sounds, the braying of donkeys, the thin wailing of flutes, the distant beating of drums, the babble and chatter of the streets.

Above all, the words. Seymour had an unusually acute ear for language and now he was quite dazed. All morning he had been speaking French. That was all right, he spoke it well; but the suddenness and totality of his immersion in it was rather disorienting.

And then the odd mixture of French and Arabic! The shopkeepers, the people you heard talking as they passed you in the streets – they all spoke French. Even Mustapha and Idris habitually spoke French. But the poorer people, the workmen, the men sweeping up the donkey dung, spoke Arabic. Seymour spoke some Arabic, he had picked it up in Istanbul, but that was a different Arabic from this. Yet he felt its undertone beneath the French, continuously there in the background.

The words continued to dance in his mind now, both Arabic and French, all jumbled together, as he lay there on his bed, watching the ripples of sunlight playing on the ceiling, reflected somehow from the bay, the words, but also the things, all mixed up: the French soldiers wearing Bedouin headdresses, the shopkeepers, with their polite, cultivated French, but sitting on the counters. Everything all jumbled up, all mixed. France and Africa.

Macfarlane came punctually at five. There were some people he should see 'in order to clear things'. First, as etiquette demanded, the People of the Parasol.

'You know about the Royal Parasol? No? Well, whenever the Sultan goes out, a slave goes with him holding the Royal Parasol over his head. It is a splendid affair, all blue and green and glittering, like a peacock's tail. Everything beneath it is, as it were, in the shade conferred by the Sultan. And so a saying has grown up: "Under the Parasol." What is under the Sultan's protection. Meaning Morocco. No longer, I'm afraid.'

They were going, he said, to see the Vizier for the Interior, Suleiman Fazi.

'There are several Viziers: for Foreign Affairs, Trade, War – you remember Sheikh Musa? He was Vizier for War until he resigned in protest over the Sultan's agreement to the French establishing a Protectorate. The Viziers are like Ministers and they have that standing. Together they form the Mahzen, the Sultan's Government.'

Suleiman Fazi offered them mint tea – mint tea, Seymour soon learned, was the staple of Moroccan social life – which was served at a low table in the ante-room to his office. He seemed in no hurry to turn to business and Macfarlane was too experienced in Moroccan ways to attempt to press him. For some time the conversation was confined to inquiries about their respective families.

'And how is Awad?' asked Macfarlane. 'He must have finished his law studies now.'

'He has, yes.'

'Satisfactorily, I hope?'

'Oh, yes. No worries on that score. He's a bright lad.'

'And what is he going to do now?'

'That, alas, remains to be seen.'

'Something in the Mahzen?'

'He's not keen.'

Macfarlane looked surprised.

'I would have thought, with his advantages –'

'Oh, something could be found. Has, indeed, been offered. But – he is thinking of working elsewhere.'

'Elsewhere?'

'In another country.'

Suleiman Fazi looked unhappy.

'Morocco, of course, is not as it was,' he said quietly. 'The Sultan keeps his Parasol, but nothing under it remains the same.'

'And Awad doesn't like that? He's not happy about the Protectorate?'

'He is thinking of leaving.'

'Of leaving Morocco? But where would he go to?'

'Ah,' said Suleiman Fazi, 'that is the question.'

'Algeria?'

'French,' said Suleiman Fazi.

'Tunisia? Libya?'

'French, too.'

'Egypt?'

'English. It is a question,' said Suleiman Fazi, 'that he has not yet resolved.'

'It would be a pity if he left,' said Macfarlane. 'People like him will be needed here.'

'That is what I tell him. To be like you, he says? There are worse fates, I say. Oh, he says? Tell me them.'

'The young are always restive,' said Macfarlane.

'There is nothing for him here,' said Suleiman Fazi. 'There is nothing for me, either. All the French will let us do,' he said bitterly, 'is collect the taxes for them. And you can imagine how popular that makes us! Everything else we have to leave to the French.'

He looked at Seymour.

'Your concern is with Bossu,' he said. 'Our concern is with the hundreds of Bossus that will be coming.'

'He means: under the Protectorate?' said Seymour.

'Yes. He fears that the French will flood in. As they have done in Algeria.'

'And will they?'

'The army first. First they have to secure the country. Which, of course, they are presently doing. And that is why I am taking you now to see Monsieur Lambert, the Resident-General Designate.'

'Ah!' said Monsieur Lambert. '*L'affaire Bossu*. And you are Monsieur Seymour. From Scotland Yard. A long way to

40

come, Monsieur Seymour, and I wonder if your visit is strictly necessary.'

'The committee,' said Macfarlane softly, 'is an international one, and other powers beside France need to be satisfied.'

'The committee!' said the Resident-General, brushing it aside.

'Nevertheless, it has to be worked with, Georges,' said Macfarlane quietly.

Monsieur Lambert seemed about to say something but then thought better.

'Have the Mahzen been informed?' he asked.

'I have taken Mr Seymour to see Suleiman Fazi.'

'Good.'

He turned to Seymour.

'The forms have to be preserved,' he said. 'We know they are just forms, that the Sultan and his Mahzen have no longer any real power. Nevertheless, we must keep to the forms. Pretend that he has. In the interests of –'

He stopped.

'International harmony,' prompted Macfarlane. 'The other powers wouldn't like it if the French just said, "Right, we're taking over Morocco." It would look bad. But if they say, "Look, we're just trying to help Morocco along, protect it from other nasty European powers, so we're declaring it a French Protectorate," well, that looks much better. It makes it more legitimate, and the international community likes legitimacy.'

Monsieur Lambert shrugged.

'Well, I don't mind keeping up appearances,' he said, 'if that's strictly necessary. It's as well, though, if Monsieur Seymour understands the difference between appearances and reality. And the reality is that a Frenchman has been killed and I am the one who has to answer for that in Paris.'

'Of course!' said Macfarlane soothingly. 'But it is also true that in the present delicate situation Monsieur Bossu was as well a servant of the international community and they too require satisfaction.'

'They're not going to make trouble, are they, Alan?' said Monsieur Lambert.

'Not if I can help it,' said Macfarlane.

'Bossu has caused enough trouble as it is,' said Lambert.

At the end of the corridor, as they came out, Seymour saw a small group of women about to enter the private quarters of the Residency. One of them was a middle-aged woman, the mother, perhaps, of the two younger women who were with her.

But, hold on! That couldn't be right, since one of the younger women, he was almost sure, was the receptionist at the hotel.

They disappeared inside.

'What trouble did Bossu cause?' asked Seymour, as they walked away.

'Oh, something in the past,' said Macfarlane.

'He's meeting all the nobs,' Seymour heard Idris say to Mustapha. 'That can't be good, can it?'

'So where in all this,' said Seymour, 'do the police fit in? Do they come under the Mahzen or under the French?'

'Both,' said Macfarlane. 'In principle, they report to the Vizier of the Interior. But in practice it's more complicated. In much of the interior there aren't any police at all. The only thing keeping order is the French army. In the more settled parts there will be a Pasha or a Caid – a sort of local governor. And in the big cities, Marrakesh, for instance, or Casablanca, there will be both a Pasha and a French commander.'

'I see,' said Seymour. Doubtfully.

'Remember, though,' said Macfarlane enthusiastically, 'that this is a Muslim country and wherever you are, most things will be handled by the local mosque. Disputes about property, say. In fact, most disputes. In so far as there is law in most of the country, it's Muslim law.'

'Well, I'm not very up in Muslim law –'

'Don't worry about that. You don't need to be. The local mosque comes in usually when it's a question not of law but of arbitration. Settling an argument between two parties. As long as you stay on the right side of them, you'll be all right.'

'I see,' said Seymour, even more doubtfully. And then –

'So where does Renaud fit in?'

'Ah, well, Tangier is a bit different. There are a lot of businesses here which would like more freedom than either the Sultans or the French would like to give them. International businesses, for instance. So part of the Protectorate deal was that Tangier should become an international zone, a sort of free city. There actually *is* a Chief of Police here. That's because there are a lot of European businesses and they like things to be done in the European way. Renaud is their man. In more senses than one.'

Seymour was silent for a moment. Then –

'So who is it exactly that I'm answerable to over investigating Bossu's death?'

'Me.' Macfarlane frowned. 'Although I have to say that part was left rather vague. Just take it, in practice, that you're answerable to me.'

'Oh, good. Well –'

'As well as to a lot of other people, of course. France, Spain, Italy and Germany will be taking an interest, especially as the committee is their creation and Bossu was, in a sense, their appointee. And, of course, the Mahzen. It would be improper to leave them out. And then the French – Monsieur Lambert should certainly be kept informed. The Muslims I don't think you need to bother about. You just have to stay on side with them, and that should be easy.'

'Easy? Ye-e-s . . .'

'And the same with the settlers. Mind you, they're trouble-makers, but if you handle them in the right way . . .

'And the business interests. Large business, that is. They're very important. They've got a voice in Paris. That's partly what Lambert was talking about . . . Bossu, you know . . . there was a time when he was very close to them. Perhaps he still was . . .

'Any more? No, I don't think so. I think that's about it.'

'Well, that seems straightforward,' said Seymour.

By now it was about eight o'clock and the city was just waking up. The streets in the main shopping quarter were crowded and the shops full of people. Up here, where Macfarlane had brought him, the shops were mostly European, spacious, well lit and with counters which were not sat upon but where the goods were displayed in the European way. The goods, too, were European: shoes from Spain, perfumerie and lingerie from France, elegant European dresses from Italy. You could well have been on the other side of the Mediterranean in the towns of Italy or Spain or Greece.

The shoppers, too, seemed European. At least, they were dressed in European styles. Only the occasional dark-veiled, dark-gowned woman lingered along looking in at the windows. The men were bolder, walking along in twos and threes in the middle of the street, their arms around each other in the Arab manner. Many of them, especially the younger ones, had doffed their brightly coloured gowns in favour of shirt and trousers.

Tangier was evidently changing, and it wasn't just the political change, the coming of the Protectorate, it was social change: the coming of Western ways of shopping, the abandonment of the intimate cubby holes of people

44

like Ali, the tailor, for the bright, public world of the metropolis.

He was just saying this to Macfarlane when down the middle of the street came a file of white horses. On either side of them were Arabs in short white gowns revealing brawny knees pressed tight to the sides of the horses. With them, also on a horse, was Millet, the horse doctor. He put his hand up and the cavalcade stopped.

'Hello, Millet,' said Macfarlane. 'Taking mounts to the barracks?'

'Just checking them over first,' said Millet.

He frowned, and then urged his horse out to one side.

'Will you walk that one for me a bit, Ahmet?' he called.

One of the white-gowned figures retrieved a horse from the line, swung down and then for a moment walked it up and down in front of Millet.

'There! See it? I don't like that for one moment.'

The Arab nodded.

'I will tell Sheikh Musa,' he said.

'He won't like that! Someone must have missed it. Musa's mounts are usually pretty good,' he said to Seymour. 'We don't usually have any trouble. The old man's got an eye like a hawk.'

The Arab said something.

'He says Musa will be angry. The man at the paddock should have spotted this.'

'Will you see to it, Ahmet? And explain to Sheikh Musa? He'll take your word for it. Ahmet knows nearly as much about horses as Musa does,' he said to Seymour.

The Arab obviously understood some French for there was a flash of white teeth as he grinned.

'Musa's right-hand man. We rely on him, absolutely rely on him, for the pig-sticking. He gets the pigs in position and then, once the chase has started, rides outrider on one side to check things keep all right. See if anyone's fallen off.'

'Did he see Bossu fall off?'

'He saw he had fallen off and sent someone back for the

45

horse. But that was later. Okay. Ahmet, let's get moving again!'

The file of horses continued on their way. No one took any notice of them. Sights like this were evidently not uncommon in the middle of Tangier.

Macfarlane was taking him to the committee's offices, which were in one of the big banks. A committee like the Consular Committee would normally have met in the rooms of its Chairman. The British Consulate, however, Macfarlane explained, was too small – its size an accurate reflection of the extent of Britain's interest in Morocco – and so alternative accommodation had had to be found. The French had offered a temptingly palatial suite in the offices of the Resident-General but this was felt, reluctantly, to compromise too obviously the committee's independence. The Germans, seeking to ingratiate themselves with the Sultan, had proposed somewhere within the Mahzen, but the Sultan did not recognize the committee and refused to have anything to do with it. In the end, the committee had had to settle for some rooms in the offices of one of the big foreign banks, which, so far as sending out signals was concerned, was probably the worst of all possible worlds.

Macfarlane took him up to the third floor and through a door marked Joint Inter-Consular Committee. Inside were three rooms: a large committee room, an even larger office (Bossu's) and a rather smaller one which accommodated the committee's papers and also an elderly man who rose politely from his desk when they entered.

'Hello, Mr Bahnini,' said Macfarlane. 'Still here, then?'

'I'm just sorting out the papers for the meeting tomorrow. You recall, I hope . . .?'

'Ten o'clock,' said Macfarlane. 'I'll be here. What we would do without Mr Bahnini, I don't know,' he said to Seymour. 'Mr Bahnini, can I introduce Monsieur Seymour? You remember, I said I would be bringing him round.

46

Seymour, this is Mr Bahnini, the mainstay of our committee. Especially now that Bossu has gone. He ran the office for him. Clerk to the clerk, you might say.'

Mr Bahnini smiled faintly.

'And we all know what that means. The man who does all the work.'

Mr Bahnini bowed slightly in polite acknowledgement.

'And now, for all intents and purposes, clerk. At least for the time being.'

'Actually, sir, I wished to speak to you about that.'

'Naturally, your extra duties will be remunerated.'

'No, no, sir, it wasn't that. The fact is, I was hoping to relinquish them.'

'Well, we're rather hoping that the committee won't go on for too long –'

'I was hoping to relinquish them immediately, sir.'

'That would be a shame, Robert. Just when we need continuity.'

'I am sorry, sir.'

'Got something else to go to?'

'Not exactly, sir. I was hoping to return to Casablanca.'

'Couldn't you delay your return? It will only be for a few months. We'd make it worth your while.'

'I'm afraid not, sir.'

'It would make a difference to your pension. You do have a pension, don't you?'

'A small one. From the Ministry. I worked there before joining Mr Bossu.'

'A small one. There you are! We'd step it up, you know. I'm sure you could do with some more money coming in. How's that boy of yours? Has he finished yet? Still an expense, I'll be bound.'

'He has just finished at university, sir.'

'Got anything to go to? No? Well, look here, we might even be able to find something for him. He could assist you in the office. After all, you're taking on Bossu's work, so someone will have to take on yours.'

Mr Bahnini shook his head.

'I don't think he would be interested, sir.'

'Just while he was looking around?' said Macfarlane temptingly.

'I'm afraid, sir, that for him it's a matter of principle.'

'I see. Ah, the young! Not a matter of principle for you, too, I trust?'

'No, sir. I compromised my principles long ago,' said Mr Bahnini quietly.

'Haven't we all?' said Macfarlane, sighing. 'Well, if you're really sure about this –'

'I am, sir.'

'In that case, we'll have to accept it. Give it another day or two to think it over, remembering what I said about the pension. And then if you still want it, I'll take the necessary action.'

'Thank you, sir.'

'Although how we shall manage without you, I don't know. You've been here right from the start. Bossu brought you with him, didn't he? We've always thought of you as Bossu's man.'

'That is just the trouble, sir,' said Mr Bahnini.

'Mind if I have a quick look?' said Seymour.

Mr Bahnini showed him into Bossu's office. It was full of potted palms. They were everywhere. There were two by the window, as if Bossu couldn't stand the harsh daylight, two either side of his desk, and others scattered around the room. Two were hanging over a long divan, two more stood beside easy chairs, and there was one near a low coffee table.

Seymour went over to the desk and tried it. The drawers were open but there was little of interest in them. Few papers of any kind. No desk diary, as far as he could see.

'You kept his diary?'

'In so far as one was kept. Mr Bossu didn't work by journal appointments. He liked to drop in on people, meet

48

them in hotels over a drink. It was very hard to tie him down, sir.'

Beside the desk was a filing cabinet. Seymour tried it but it was locked.

'I have the key, sir,' said Mr Bahnini.

He went out of the office and returned with a small brown envelope.

'The keys were on his person, sir, when he was found. Mr Macfarlane took charge of all his private belongings. The keys were among them. He brought them back and deposited them with me. The envelope has not been opened.'

When Seymour opened the filing cabinet he found it largely empty. There were just a few scraps of paper, leaves torn from a pad, with some notes scribbled on them. Seymour looked at them and then, for the moment, put them in his pocket.

Macfarlane had invited him home to dinner. When they got there his wife had just finished putting the children to bed. Macfarlane went up to kiss them goodnight and Mrs Macfarlane collapsed with a drink on the divan. She was a small, bright, birdlike woman, Scottish, like her husband.

'Well, Mr Seymour,' she said, 'how do you find us?'

He took her to be referring to Morocco as a whole.

'A strange mixture,' he said. 'Strange, but interesting.'

'It is that,' she said. 'And sometimes I think it's getting stranger.'

'As the French move in?'

'As the West moves in. I think I liked it more as it was. Dirty and barbarous. Often cruel. But, somehow, authentic. Itself.'

'You liked it under the Parasol?'

She laughed.

'Life under the Parasol was not that special,' she said drily. 'Especially at court. Diplomats see a lot of courts, and they're not always the most interesting places to see. When

49

we came out here first the Sultan was very young. Just a child, really. And he made the whole court a nursery, a kind of playroom, as my parents would have called it.

'At one time he developed a craze for bicycle polo. Bicycles were a new thing then. He got the whole court to play, even the Viziers. Even –' she laughed – 'some of the Consuls. My husband, for instance. Although he quite liked it. Actually, I would like to have played, myself. We used to play it as children at home. But, of course, as a woman I wouldn't do it here. The court became very indulgent but not quite that indulgent! This is, after all, a Muslim country.

'And, as in many Eastern countries, the Sultan had absolute power. Even if he was just a child. And because his power was absolute, he thought he could do anything. They all had to obey his will. And if his will was to play bicycle polo all day, well, so be it.

'He had no sense of – well, measure. For example, they were always smashing the bicycles up. Well, that was no problem. He would just order the Vizier to get new ones. And everything was like that. Money was no object. If he suddenly felt he wanted something, he would just get it. Money simply ran through his fingers. He thought it would never run out. But, of course, it did. And that enabled the French to come in. It's always like that. It was just the same in Egypt under the old Khedive when we were there.'

'He's still like that, is he?'

'Less so now. The French have hemmed him in. Controlled his expenditure. And, besides, he's grown up a bit. But it's too late. He's lost all his support. His capriciousness has turned everybody against him. Even his own half-brother.'

She sighed.

'So you see,' she said, 'it wasn't always that good under the Parasol. I liked it as it was but maybe it had to change. And you could have worse people coming in than the French. I sometimes think that the French and the

Moroccans have a lot in common. Their cultures are more traditional than ours, more formal, more polite, naturally courteous. When you go to a French household the children come round before going to bed to shake hands. In a Moroccan family it's rather like that, too. Whereas with my savages . . .!'

Macfarlane came downstairs and they went out into a little courtyard to dine. The house was an old Arab one, with a courtyard almost inside the house and boxed wooden windows looking down on it from above. A fountain played into a small pond and around the walls were cypresses and jasmine. As it grew darker the smell of the jasmine was joined by the scents of other flowers which opened only at night.

The meal was Arab, too, with hot, peppery soup and then various kinds of meats, served with rice and burning hot peppers. Afterwards, there was melon and iced orgeat, made of crushed almonds, milk and sugar.

Seymour was a little surprised. In his office Macfarlane had seemed so British. At home he seemed much more responsive to things Moroccan. Perhaps that was the effect of his job. More likely, thought Seymour, it was the effect of his wife.

She asked him if the hotel was comfortable.

'Very,' he said. 'And the people are most helpful.' He mentioned the receptionist.

'Chantale,' said Mrs Macfarlane, with a smile.

'She seems very versatile.'

'Aye, she is that,' said Macfarlane.

'She has to be,' said Mrs Macfarlane. 'She and her mother run that hotel between them and there can't be a lot of money to spare.'

'She's a good lassie,' Macfarlane conceded.

'A journalist, too, you said,' said Seymour.

'She would like to be. But it's not easy if you're a woman and in an Arab country.'

'She writes mostly for the French newspapers,' said Mrs Macfarlane.

'It's still not easy.'

'She seems to have good French contacts,' said Seymour. 'I saw her with the pig-sticking crowd and then again, I think, at the Resident-General's.'

'She would have been going to see Cecile,' said Mrs Macfarlane.

'Cecile?'

'The Lamberts' daughter. They were at school together.'

'Not altogether happily in Chantale's case,' said Macfarlane.

'She rebelled against it. It was a convent school and too strict for her. So soon after her father's death. But what could they do? There aren't many schools here and they wanted it to be a French one. The Lamberts were very good to her. They treated her like another daughter. She's always been very close to them.'

'She wanted to be independent, though.'

Mrs Macfarlane laughed.

'She would, wouldn't she? But it's a good thing they got that hotel. It gives them a base of their own, and you need that if you're a woman in Morocco.'

'Aye, but will it do for her in the long run?'

'Why shouldn't it?'

'You always feel that she's champing at the bit.'

'Isn't that inevitable?'

'She ought to go to France,' said Macfarlane.

'But would that work out any better? It would be the same thing only the other way round.'

'Sorry?' said Seymour.

'Perhaps you've not understood,' said Mrs Macfarlane. 'Chantale is half Moroccan.'

Chapter Four

The next morning, it seemed that all Tangier was on the
road: except that when they got to the Tent it seemed as if
all Tangier had already got there. The space around the
marquee was packed with people, hundreds, perhaps
thousands, of them, many of them dressed in robes of pink
and blue, saffron and mauve. The Tent, too, was already
full of people. A long bar ran down one side of it and there
was a crush of people six feet deep pressed against it.
Away from the bar it was almost as crowded.

Macfarlane took one look and said: 'We'd better go
straight to the enclosure.'

Behind the Tent was a roped-off enclosure full of horses
and men, the men in brightly coloured shirts and riding
breeches, and holding lances, the horses nervous and
frisky. Apart from the lances it reminded Seymour of . . .
What was it? A circus? That County Show again? He'd got
it! He knew what it was. As part of the show there had
been a gymkhana. That was it: it reminded him of a
gymkhana.

What followed, though, was not at all like a gymkhana.

A bugle sounded and anyone in the enclosure who was
not already on a horse began to mount. There were about
a hundred riders and now they were all holding lances,
their points held vertical, as in a Renaissance painting.

A rope was removed and the horses began to move
round the side of the marquee and out towards the desert
and scrub.

The crowd surged with them, small boys running excitedly ahead and frequently in front of the horses. The horses took no notice. They formed into a long line and began to trot.

The crowd, too, began to trot, and Seymour, willy-nilly, with them. People pressed in upon him on all sides. He very soon lost sight of Macfarlane. He found himself being carried along and began to feel anxious. Crowd control? Where was it? They were all running. If one person went down it would be a disaster.

Horses and people were making for a point in the distance where a man holding a flag stood on a large box.

Seymour fought to remain upright.

Suddenly he felt his arms grasped. Mustapha was on one side, Idris on the other. For the first time he was glad of their support.

The crowd had quietened down. Everyone, like him, was concentrating on running. It was like being in a marathon.

The horses quickened their pace and drew ahead of the runners. The small boys scattered. The man on the box raised his flag. Just as the line of riders was about to reach it, he dropped it.

The horses shot away and the crowd surged after them. Away in the distance Seymour could see shapes moving in the scrub. Around them were men in white robes on horses, Musa's men. The pigs began to run.

Everyone was shouting excitedly. The horses were away out in front and the crowd beginning to stretch out behind them. Some of the fleetest runners were well ahead. Presumably the less fleet were already well behind. Seymour was in the middle, stumbling along, half-supported, half-carried by Idris and Mustapha.

'Come on, come on!' they shouted.

A few of the pigs ran off to one side and one or two of the riders went after them. Seymour tried to pull across.

'What are you doing? This way!'

'No, I want to —'

54

'This way, Monsieur! On ahead! Look!'

'Yes, but I don't want to –'

'Come on, Monsieur! What are you *doing*?'

'This way! Straight ahead! Look, you can see –'

'Yes, but I want to go that way!'

'Monsieur, can't you *see*?'

'Come on, come on!'

The line of horsemen, too, had broken up. Some were already far in the distance. Behind them, riding in a group, were some men he recognized. The soldiers! In their head-dresses! They were riding in a compact, disciplined way, their lances all at the same angle.

'This way! Monsieur, Monsieur –'

'No, I want to go –'

'But, Monsieur!'

'There they are! That way! See?'

'No, no, it's the others I want to go after.'

He managed to pull out of the flow and over to one side.

'What are you *doing*?' cried Mustapha, almost stamping in vexation.

'Some pigs ran off this way. And a few of the riders went after them.'

'Yes, I know. But –'

'Just as Bossu did.'

'Bossu?'

Mustapha stopped.

'You know, Monsieur,' he said, 'you disappoint me.'

Ahead of him in the scrub he could see a group of horse-men. They had come to a stop and were arranged in a small circle.

He walked through the bushes towards them. He could see them clearly. On their horses they stood out above the scrub. They were all looking down and the points of their lances were down.

'Its too late, Monsieur, you've got here too *late*,' said Idris. 'You've missed it.'

Seymour ignored him.

'We should have stayed with the others. It's true we'd have missed it with them, too, you always do when you're on foot. But there would have been more of them, you'd have seen more –'

'He's thinking about Bossu,' said Mustapha.

'Why didn't we stay with the others?' grumbled Idris. 'You've missed all the fun.' He stopped. 'Bossu?'

'The Frenchman,' said Mustapha.

'Well, that's not very exciting, is it? We should have stayed with –'

There was a sudden crashing in the bushes and the next moment a pig darted out.

'Jesus!'

It rushed towards them.

Several things happened at once. There was the sound of a shot and the squeal of a pig and Seymour was sent sprawling.

When he looked up there were men coming towards him with lances at the ready. They reined in.

'What are you doing? You've shot our pig!'

'Too bloody true I've shot your pig!' said Mustapha.

'Fool!'

'Idiot!'

'What are you doing here? And what are *you* doing here?' asked someone, catching sight of Seymour. 'Don't you know –?'

'Yes, yes,' said Seymour. 'The pig ran out upon us.'

'You oughtn't to be here. This is –'

'I know, I know.'

'Yes, but he shot it! He shouldn't have done that!'

'It was coming for us. He had to act quickly.'

'Yes, but you don't shoot pigs!'

'What do you expect me to do?' asked Mustapha. 'Strangle it?'

'What are you doing here, anyway? You shouldn't be here. You're just a –'

'I can see one!' shouted one of the horsemen excitedly. 'Over there!'

'Where? Where?'

'This way, this way –'

They rode off.

'Exciting enough for you now?' asked Seymour.

They left the shot pig lying and walked over to where the men had made their kill. The stuck pig was lying on its side in a little clearing. It had been killed by a single thrust and a trickle of blood ran down into the sand from between its shoulders. Already the flies were gathering.

Seymour walked round it, trying to take in as much as he could. Later, a particular detail might become relevant. At the moment he could only stare.

Mustapha and Idris sat in the shade of a bush, bored.

'Seen what you want, Monsieur?' hinted Idris, after a while.

The truth was, there wasn't much to see. A dead pig looked, well, like a dead pig.

Men were coming through the bushes on foot. They were Musa's men and their job was to collect the pigs after they had been stuck. They had brought poles with them which they thrust between the pigs' trotters after they had tied them together. They did this to both pigs, the shot one as well as the stabbed one. Then they hoisted the poles on to their shoulders and with the pigs slung beneath set off back to the Tent.

Quite a crowd had gathered round, Seymour suddenly realized, to watch. They were mostly the ones unable to keep up with the hunt: the old, the fat, the halt and the lame.

A thought struck him. They would have been old and fat and lame on the previous occasion, too.

He began to move among them.

'Were you here when the Frenchman . . .? Did you see . . .?'

They looked at him blankly.

He had tried them in French. Up to now he had found that everyone in Morocco spoke French. Now, of course, it appeared that no one did.

He tried them in his less strong Arabic.

'Pig-stuck?' said a man helpfully, but then lapsed into silence.

'Here?'

There was no response. He couldn't believe that no one, absolutely no one, seemed to understand him. What he needed was an interpreter, or at least someone who could put the questions for him. Surely, among all these people, there was someone who . . .

His eye fell on Mustapha and Idris.

'Listen,' he said.

'Hello!' said Macfarlane. 'Given up the chase?'

'I've seen what I need.'

'Already? But you'll have missed the exciting bit at the end!'

'So did Bossu,' said Seymour.

At the far end of the bar he saw Madame Bossu, surrounded by men all anxious to help her make up for her loss. He had no wish to add to their numbers but the sight of her put into his mind another of Bossu's women, the *petite amie* who lived in town. Monique, was that her name?

He saw Millet, the horse doctor, and went up to him.

'Monique? Yes, I expect she's here. Would you like me to introduce you?'

She was another blonde, not, this time, pouting and fluffy but thin-faced and harder, as if the sun and the wind had worn her youth away.

'Monique, can I present Monsieur Seymour? He is from England and has come here to look into Bossu's death.'

'He is more likely to get somewhere than Renaud is.' She extended her hand. 'I am pleased to meet you, Monsieur.'

'You have been in the country long?'

'All my life.'

'You will know it well, then. And, of course, you knew Bossu.'

'Of course.'

'Could you tell me something about him?'

'I don't know that I can tell you anything that will help you on this –'

'In general, then. Tell me about him as a man.'

She laughed.

'As a man? Well, there I could tell you a lot!'

'I have no wish to pry, Madame, but it would help me if I could get a picture of him. As a person. I know nothing about him, you see.'

'Where to begin!' She thought. 'Well, why not! Everyone else knows, so why shouldn't you? I will begin with me. Let me tell you the story of my life. It is a very ordinary story, the old story of a rich man and a poor girl.

'My parents were settlers. They came out here to farm. And, like most settlers, they struggled. We were poor. We came out here to make our fortune but instead we lost it. So you can understand that my parents did not dissuade a rich neighbour when he began to pay attention to me. I was beautiful then.

'No, don't say I am beautiful still. That is the sort of thing all men say. And it is not true. This country is hard on women. But I was beautiful then and I caught Bossu's eye. He had bought some property nearby. He began to pay attention to me and I was flattered. No, more; I was bowled over. I was, after all, only fifteen.

'And my parents did not dissuade him. Even when they learned that he was already married. They were poor, you understand? Desperate. And he was a rich man. Very rich, for Tangier. So they did not dissuade him. And they didn't say anything after he bought me an apartment in Tangier and I moved into it.

'Well, that's it. You asked me about Bossu, Bossu, the man. Does that tell you something about Bossu, the man?'

'Yes, it does.'

'Since he died, I have had time to think things over. And I realize that to him I was never more than a possession. Like the farm he bought next to my parents' farm. He liked possessions. But he never did anything with them. He never built on them. I had hoped, when he put me in that flat, that one day we might build something together. But we never did. He wasn't that kind of man. He never built anything. Not even in business.'

'Not even in business?'

'He wasn't that kind of businessman. What he did was to bring people together. He knew everybody, not just in Tangier but all over the country. If you were a business which wanted to develop the interior, build railways, say, or roads, he knew who to put you in touch with. The local Caid, local contractors, local sheikhs. Bossu would always know someone who could help you. That is important in a country like this where everything is personal. If you wanted to do something, Bossu could make it possible. He became also indispensable.

'But, of course, things could go wrong. He worked with a lot of people, and some of them weren't very nice people. There were people in the interior who were little better than bandits. And there were developers from the city who were ruthless. He put them together and that could lead to – as in Casablanca. You know about Casablanca?'

'No.'

'There was trouble there. Big trouble. About five or six years ago. It was to do with a quarry and a railway. Bossu had put the two together in some project. Things went wrong and there were riots. It was very bad. The army was sent in and they killed a lot of people.

'But some say that that was the idea. To get the city to

60

explode, so that the army would have to step in, and then France could take over the whole country. I don't know if that is true, but that is what people say. And the Moroccans believe it.

'So Casablanca and what happened there is very big to Moroccans. And Bossu was right in the middle of it. I don't know exactly how he was involved but I know that he was involved. This was six years ago and I was still young. I did not understand these things. But I remember him coming home and saying, "This will either make me or break me." Afterwards, he thought it had made him.'

She laughed.

'They all trusted him, you see, after that. Trust! Bossu!'

She laughed again.

'They used him more and more. All over the country. Whenever there was something big. Because they thought they could rely on him to look after their interests.'

'Was that why he was put on the committee?'

'Of course! The big businessmen all knew him and they wanted someone like him in a big position on the committee so that he could look after their interests. And the settlers, too. They thought: he is one of us, he will see that things don't go wrong.

'But perhaps – perhaps something *did* go wrong. And perhaps . . . Perhaps he was right. On both counts. It did make him, yes; but in the end it broke him. I don't know. I don't know about these things.'

She looked at him over the top of her glass, weighing it, considering.

'But, shall I tell you something? I liked being possessed. Women do. And now that I am no longer possessed, I feel . . . disoriented. Not bereft. He never loved me and I never loved him. Just disoriented. But free.'

Chantale was over on the other side of the Tent talking to Sheikh Musa. Seymour was a little surprised. He didn't know how it was in Morocco, or how Sheikh Musa was, but you wouldn't have seen this in Istanbul, nor, he suspected, in many other Muslim countries. A woman talking so familiarly to a man. But, of course, she was half French, too. Perhaps it was the French half that Musa was addressing. And yet . . . and yet they were both drinking lemonade. That was a Muslim thing to do. Curious. Not just curious: intriguing.

She saw him looking at her and waved a hand. Shortly afterwards she detached herself from Sheikh Musa and came across to him.

'I see you've caught up with Monique?'

'Yes.'

'How did you find her?'

'Interesting. And rather nice.'

'She *is*.' She seemed pleased. 'She should never have got hooked up with Bossu.'

'It was Bossu we were talking about.'

'Of course. And what did she tell you?'

'A bit about herself. And a lot about Bossu.'

'What did she tell you about Bossu?'

'We talked generally,' he said guardedly.

Chantale laughed.

'Well, if you find out something particular, come and tell me. I, too, am interested in Bossu. Perhaps we could do a trade? You tell me what you find out and I'll tell you what I know.'

'I might take you up on that.'

'Please do. What you tell me doesn't have to appear in the newspaper. My interest in Bossu is a private one.'

'I'll bear that in mind.'

She smiled and moved away. Afterwards he found himself wondering about her. She had hazel eyes. Or would you call them green?

The heat in the Tent, and the noise, was almost unbearable. He made his way to the back and then out into the enclosure. Millet and Meunier were standing there with drinks in their hands: not lemonade.

'What's it been like for you today?' he asked. 'Busy?'

'Quiet. A fall or two, but nothing serious.'

The riders were returning now. De Grassac went past, leading a horse.

'How is Sybille?' asked Millet.

'Oh, fine. Fine.'

'She always goes very well,' said Millet.

He had taken them to be referring to de Grassac's wife, or girlfriend, perhaps; but maybe not.

'How many did you get?' asked Meunier.

'Two. Better than the last time. I got nowhere last time. By the time I got there, there was always someone ahead of me.'

'How many were killed altogether today?' asked Seymour.

'Ten, I think. Including one shot one.'

'Shot one?' said de Grassac, puzzled. 'That can't be right!'

Meunier's eyes met Seymour's neutrally.

'So two is pretty good,' said Millet. 'De Grassac's an expert.'

'Boileau is better than me,' said de Grassac modestly, 'and Levret is coming along, don't you think?'

'He got two today.'

'That's good for someone with so little experience. He's only been out here six months.'

'I thought he spent all his time hunting women?'

'Most of it. But he hunts pigs as well.'

Mustapha and Idris arrived at this point, limping.

'Two more for you,' Seymour said to Meunier.

'Oh, I don't treat pedestrians.'

Seymour took them aside and they sank gratefully to the ground.

'How did you get on?'

'No one saw a thing,' said Mustapha, depressed.

'No one saw a thing?'

'They all got there afterwards. When word got round.'

'No one followed him in? When they saw he'd gone after the pig?'

'Well, one of them had. He hadn't wanted to. He had seen at once what the Frenchman was like. From the moment he turned aside. Couldn't stick a cow, he said. Even if its legs were tied together. So he'd said, "Let's give this one a miss." But the man he was with had insisted. Thought they'd get right up close. Not a chance! Complete waste of time!'

'But he must have seen something.'

'Not much. When he got there it was all over. There was the Frenchman lying on the ground. He thought at first it was a fall. But then he saw the lance. Didn't know what to make of it. But the man he was with said it was bad and that they should keep out of it. He'd seen that it was a Frenchman, you see, and worked out that someone would be over pretty soon. And that someone would probably be the French army, and that wouldn't be good at all. So they kept out of it. Just sat there to see what happened.'

'Well, what happened?'

'Nothing. Like I told you. By and by two big blokes came riding up, swords and knives bristling all over. And they told everybody to get back. I mean by this time there was quite a crowd there and they'd all crept in. Well, you can understand it, can't you? It's not every day you see a dead Frenchman and they wanted to have a good look. But these two big blokes whipped out their swords and everybody jumped back in a flash. And one of them went off and came back with another Frenchman, and he was a soldier. Just like his mate had said. So they did right to keep out of it.'

'Yes, yes, I've got that bit. But did you talk to people? Had anyone seen anything more than this chap had?'

'Of course we talked to people! But they'd all got there afterwards. Like I said.'

'There was that boy, Mustapha,' said Idris.

64

'The beggar boy, you mean? The lame one? The one with the limp.'

'That's right.'

'Well, he was the bright one. He'd know he couldn't run, so he'd gone out *before*. Before the hunt started. He'd gone out and lay down under a thorn bush so that he would see as they went past.'

'And did he see them?'

'Oh, yes.'

'Including Bossu?'

'Yes. He'd seen him go after the pig, and he'd thought, he'll never get anywhere –'

'Yes, yes. But he did see him? He saw him separate from the others. And then what?'

'He suddenly disappeared! So he reckoned he'd had a fall. Well, he waited a bit to see if he got up, but when he didn't, he thought he'd go over. I mean, you never know what you might pick up. A wallet, even.'

'So he went over there? To the spot where he'd seen Bossu fall? And what did he see?'

'Just him and the lance.'

'Did he see anyone? Anyone else?'

'He didn't say so.'

'Look, he *must* have seen someone else. The person who stuck the lance through him.'

'He didn't say –'

'Riding away?' suggested Seymour hopefully. 'Whoever did it would have been on horseback. A horse is big – no?'

'Look,' said Mustapha, wearying, 'why don't *you* ask him?'

'I will. What's his name?'

'Name?'

'He's got a name, hasn't he?'

'No. He's just a beggar boy.'

'Where does he live?'

'I've *told* you. He's a beggar boy. He doesn't live anywhere.'

'How will I find him, then, to talk to him?'

'Oh, you'll find him. He's always around.'

'Yes, he's always around,' said Idris.

As detectives, thought Seymour ruefully, they had their limitations.

He went back into the Tent. It wasn't quite as densely packed as before but the bar was still doing a roaring – and how! – trade. Suddenly, however, as if some mysterious signal had been given, all the soldiers detached themselves and made for the door at the back of the Tent. That left a number of spaces at the bar and in one of them, left bereft of her admirers, he saw Madame Bossu. She looked round, saw him and brightened.

'Monsieur Seymour!'

'Madame!'

'And how do you like our little games?'

'I find your little games enchanting, Madame.'

'That was *not* what I meant!' she said, tapping his hand reprovingly.

'But where have all your admirers gone? Earlier in the afternoon I couldn't have hoped to get near you.'

'Ah, those boys! I love the military, you know. I often used to say to Bossu, "Bossu, why aren't you a soldier?" "If I was one, you'd soon notice the difference," he would say. "Soldiers don't make any money." "You are always thinking about money," I used to tell him. "It's just as well one of us is," he would say. That wasn't very kind of him, was it?'

'Indeed not!'

'And if I spent money, he would encourage me! "Just add it to your account," he would say. So that's what I did. Add it to my accounts. All of them.'

'All of them?'

'Well, I didn't just use one dressmaker. I liked to use several. One mustn't let oneself fall into a groove.'

'Certainly not! And – and Bossu encouraged you in this?'

'He was always very generous in that way. "Don't bother your pretty little head," he would say. "Just give me the bills." So I did.'

'And he would settle them?'

'I imagine so. I never heard any more about it.'

'He would write a cheque, I imagine.'

'Cheque?'

'A little bit of paper. It's usually got a bank's name on it.'

Juliette wasn't sure about that. He certainly had a lot of little bits of paper. And, yes, he used to write on them sometimes.

'You don't remember the name on the bit of paper, do you? The bank's name?'

Juliette's smooth forehead wrinkled.

'There were a lot of names,' she said doubtfully.

'One in particular?'

Juliette couldn't recall.

'I think he used a lot of banks,' she said. And then, helpfully: 'Like me, dressmakers.'

'And when he wanted cash, to give to you, say, what did he do?'

'Do you know,' said Juliette, 'I've never asked myself that. I would just ask and he would always give me some.'

'Where did he keep it?'

'Keep it?'

'Did he have a safe or something? A drawer, perhaps? in his desk?'

'Not that I've found,' said Juliette. 'And I've looked.'

Her eyes widened.

'My God!' she said. 'You don't think . . .'

'What?'

'That he kept it at Monique's! That bitch! She must have it all!'

'No, no, no! Not necessarily. He may have kept it somewhere else. And his papers, too. Did he have an office somewhere, perhaps? Apart from the one at the committee?'

67

'No, I don't think so.'

'You see, what I'm trying to do is track down any transactions he might have been engaged in. In case they throw any light, you know, on his death. I've been through his office at the committee and there didn't seem much there. Did he bring stuff like that home?'

'He brought some things home, certainly.'

'Papers?'

Juliette couldn't remember.

'Bank statements?'

What were they?

'Well . . .'

Juliette wasn't sure. She didn't think so.

'I wonder, perhaps, if you would allow me to go through his things?'

'Of course! Come round and see me,' said Juliette, brightening. 'Sometime.'

'It's just the papers,' said Seymour hastily. 'If I could.'

'I will show you everything!'

'Thank you. Yes, thank you.'

She frowned.

'Of course . . .'

'Yes?'

'Renaud has them. He's been helping me, you see. With all the – you know, the horrid stuff that has to be gone into when someone dies. He took everything away with him.'

'The papers?'

'And the bank statements,' said Juliette. 'I remember them now.'

Chapter Five

The next morning Seymour went up to the committee's offices, where he found Mr Bahnini, head down, already at work.

He took out the scraps of paper he had found in Bossu's filing cabinet and laid them on the desk in front of him.

'Could you tell me, Mr Bahnini, to what these refer?'

'They are names of places. Azrou, Immauzer and Tafilalet. And, of course, Casablanca.'

'Anything special about them?'

'The first three are in the south. They are small towns in the interior.'

'Anything else about them?'

Mr Bahnini shook his head.

'I would say there is very little to distinguish them. Apart from being the only towns in miles and miles of desert.'

'Beside them are some numbers. And dates. Azrou, for instance: 5000, 2nd April. Immauzer, 7000, 20th May. What do the numbers refer to? Could they be sums of money?'

'They could.'

'There wouldn't be any reference to these sums, if they are sums, in the minutes of the committee? I was just wondering if they were authorized expenditure.'

Mr Bahnini shook his head.

'They would not be,' he said definitely. 'The committee is not authorized to disburse funds. It has a few for expenses, of course. For stationery, my salary, and so on, but there are all minor and do not correspond to any of these sums.'

'Perhaps they're not money, then.'

Mr Bahnini studied them.

'Although what else could they be?' he said.

'Take a look at the dates. Do they correspond to anything in Bossu's diary?'

'He didn't keep one,' said Mr Bahnini. 'But I did.'

He produced a desk diary and began to go through it.

'He was certainly away from the office on those dates,' he said.

'So they could be dates of meetings?'

'But why would he have been having meetings in places like that? Casablanca, I could understand. But Tafilalet! Mr Bossu had business dealings all over the place, it is true, but – Tafilalet! It's just an oasis.'

'No record here, then?'

'No. Of course . . .'

'Yes?'

'He had business dealings of his own. He only worked for the committee part time. The sums might relate to them.'

'Where would I find out about them? Did he have another office somewhere?'

'I don't think so, sir.'

'His bank, perhaps, might have a record of cash transactions. Do you know which bank he used?'

'I am afraid not, sir. His wife, perhaps . . .'

'Doesn't know a thing. And Renaud has taken all his papers away. I could ask him, I suppose.'

Mr Bahnini was hesitating. He cleared his throat deferentially.

'I wonder, sir . . .'

'Yes?'

'I am not sure, sir, that, given the location of the places, he would have made much use of his bank. In the south they usually prefer money in physical form.'

'Coin, you mean?'

'Or bullion. Silver is much in use.'

'And if Bossu was making payments there, that is what he would have used?'

'There are no banks there, sir. The south is a very backward place. Not to say lawless.'

'Hmm. So if he wanted money in hard form, where could he have gone to get it?'

'I suspect the big moneylenders in the souk, sir. But a bank here would be able to advise you.'

'Thank you. I'll try them.'

'There is one other thing, sir.'

'Yes?'

'Money in that form is heavy. The first part of the journey could be done by truck, but after that he would have had to use camels. And porters. Also . . .'

'Yes?'

'Almost certainly he would have needed bodyguards. The south is, as I have said, a lawless place.'

Seymour asked if he could see the committee's minutes. He settled himself at Bossu's desk and Mr Bahnini brought them to him. Then he ploughed systematically through them. There was no mention of any of the places on the slips of paper, nor any reference to the dates or sums. He began to get, however, a sense of the committee's preoccupations. Impressed by his display of clerical adhesiveness, Mr Bahnini warmed to him and dropped in from time to time to explain particular points.

Much of the most recent discussion referred to a venture at Marrakesh. Mr Bahnini said that this was to do with a project to build a railway, which, it was hoped, would open up the interior. Of course, Marrakesh was a long way inland and since it did not fall within the area of the proposed Tangier zone it was, strictly speaking, nothing to do with the committee. Tangier interests would, however, be providing the money and for that reason were interested in the legal powers that the committee would be recommending. Strongly interested, judging by the frequency of the committee's returns to the subject.

'They are interested, of course, in the likely route the railway would take.'

'Is that the responsibility of the committee to decide?'

'No, but what they decide – the scope and nature of the legal powers they decide on – could have a considerable bearing on the route. That is terribly important, of course, because once the route has been decided on, businesses will be jostling to take appropriate action.'

'Appropriate?'

'Well, they would be able to plan ahead.'

'Buy land, you mean?'

'That sort of thing, yes, sir.'

'And Bossu being close to the committee's deliberations . . .'

'I must insist, sir, that anything he did would be separate from his work on the committee. The Chairman is a stickler for propriety. But, of course, outside the committee room –'

'And close as he was not just to the committee's working but also to the interests of other parties –'

'He would be well placed,' said Mr Bahnini.

'Thank you, Mr Bahnini. I think I understand what you are telling me.'

At one point Seymour heard Mr Bahnini talking to someone in his office. They kept their voices down and he couldn't hear what they were saying, but they appeared to be having an argument. The other person seemed to be a young man. After a time he went away.

When Mr Bahnini next came in to see how Seymour was getting on, he appeared vexed.

'An awkward customer?'

'Very. My son.'

'The one you were talking about with Macfarlane?'

'The same.'

'The one who has just finished his studies and is uncertain what to do?'

'It is not that he is uncertain. He doesn't appear to want to do *anything*. He just sits in the café all day with his friends listening to music.'

'He probably finds it hard to put student life behind him.'

'They all do. But it's time they did. They can't sit around for ever.'

'You couldn't tempt him to take up Macfarlane's offer? As a temporary expedient?'

'That's just what I've been trying to do. But he will have none of it. The committee is just a cover for the French, he says, and he refuses to have anything to do with it. He won't work for the Mahzen because he says it's too corrupt. All right, what about business, then, I say? There are plenty of jobs there if only you could be bothered to look for them. That would be working for foreigners, he says, and he doesn't want to do that.'

'What does he want to do?'

'Sit around in the café and chat. And his friends are just the same. They say they will only work for Morocco. Look, this *is* Morocco, I say: here! No, it's not, they say. It's France or Spain or some other rich country.

'"It's all very well for you to talk," I say to him, "but before you start taking a high-and-mighty line about principle, you've got to find a way to live. At the moment you're living on me!"

'That always makes him angry, and my wife says I mustn't say things like that. But it's true. And it's true for the others, too.

'Take young Awad. He spends all his time lolling about in the café, too, but he can do it only because his father is rich – his father is a Minister in the Mahzen, Suleiman Fazi. Did you say you had been to see him? I met him once, he's a nice man and he's just as worried about Awad as I am about Sadiq.

'I don't know what's come over the young. They have

chances we never had. And what do they do? Loll about and complain! Say the world's all wrong and that it needs to change before they'll get their hands dirty by working in it!'

Seymour laughed.

'The young have always been like that,' he said.

'But it's different now. Here. And with the Protectorate being imposed, it's become worse. They say such wild things!'

'It's just talk.'

'So long as it stops at just talk,' said Mr Bahnini darkly.

When Seymour left, he saw just such a group of young men as they had been discussing sitting in a café across the road. In fact, they *were* the young men they had been talking about, or some of them were, for as he and Mr Bahnini came out of the bank one of them looked up and saw them and then came running across the road towards them.

'Your pardon, Father,' he said. 'I spoke too warmly.'

'Like father, like son,' said Mr Bahnini. 'I spoke too warmly, too.'

The young man fell in alongside them.

'This is Monsieur Seymour,' said Mr Bahnini. 'From England.'

'Oh, from England?'

He asked Seymour, as they all did, how he found Morocco: but he asked in a different way from the others. He asked with a fierce interest, as if the answer really mattered. Seymour, who found the question difficult to answer at any depth, replied as best he could. The young man pondered and then said:

'Do you find us backward?'

'Different,' said Seymour. 'Not backward.'

'Yes, we are different,' said the young man. He appeared relieved.

Seymour said that he found Tangier different, too, from other places around the Mediterranean that he had been in; from Istanbul, for example, where he had been the previous year.

'You have been in Istanbul?'

'Briefly.'

'That is somewhere where things are happening!' said the young man enviously.

There had been a revolution there and the Sultan had been deposed.

'And how do you think it is working out?' he asked anxiously.

'It's too early to say. Things are changing, certainly. But I have a feeling that the Sultanate is not finished yet.'

'They won't go back?' said the young man, aghast.

'They might. But if they do it won't be to quite the way things were before.'

'Once change starts,' said Mr Bahnini, 'it is hard to stop it.'

'I hope that's true,' his son said. 'For Turkey's sake, at least.' He looked at Seymour. 'We have a strange situation here,' he said. 'When the revolution started in Istanbul we all said, "Yes, yes! It is a pattern for what should happen here." But it hasn't worked out like that. The French have stepped in and brought all that change to a stop.'

'Not *all* that change,' objected his father. 'Some of it will continue to go on.'

'Instead of the Sultan we have the French. That isn't much of an improvement.'

Seymour called in to see Renaud but he wasn't in his office. This was the third time Seymour had tried without success and he mentioned it to Chantale when he got back to the hotel.

'Oh, he won't be in his office!' she said.

'Where will he be, then?'

75

She looked at his watch.

'There's a little bar in the Place Concorde . . .'

And there indeed was Monsieur Renaud, perched on a stool and chatting to the *patronne*.

'*Collègue!*'

He jumped up.

'*Cher collègue!*'

They embraced.

'*Un apéritif?*'

'Allow me . . .'

And, a little later, 'Forgive me, *cher collègue*, for coming to you. It is an imposition, I know.'

'An imposition? But not at all! A pleasure! A pleasure!' Renaud repeated. He looked along the bar. The *patronne*, without saying anything, brought another two Pernods.

They exchanged toasts again.

'You know,' said Seymour, as they settled back on their stools, 'there is one thing in which I regard myself as fortunate. It is to find myself working with you.'

'Ah, Monsieur –'

'No, I mean it. It is not always that one finds oneself working with people who are so *sympathique*. Colleagues who put people first. As you so evidently do. Your solicitude for Madame Bossu! Can I say that I find it admirable? Yes, admirable. Caring, thoughtful, sensitive. One does not always find that in one's colleagues. I consider myself fortunate.'

'Ah, Monsieur, you are too kind! But you are right. For me, the human touch is all. It is not so with everybody, but for me, for me it comes first. We must not lose sight of the pain in the one who has suffered. And we must do what we can to alleviate it.'

'Just so! A man dies, and it is our job as policemen to find out who has killed him. But we must remember, too, the ones he leaves behind. The man dies and so often the woman is left alone. It is then that support is needed and, thank goodness, it is exactly that you are providing for Madame Bossu.'

'Poor Juliette!'

'She should be grateful. And I'm sure she will be. It may take a little time to show –'

'She doesn't realize all the work I am doing for her.'

'Oh, she will, she will.'

'You think so?' said Renaud, pleased.

'I am sure of it. And when she does, I am sure she will be truly grateful.'

'Well, well, that would be nice. All I want, you know, is a little appreciation.'

'And, perhaps, some time later, as she begins to recover from this terrible experience, something more? A man is a man, after all.'

'Well, yes, there is that,' said Renaud, smiling.

'Well, I wish you success! But, meanwhile there is work to be done. And a lot of it. No one knows that better than I do. Bossu was a man of so many interests. With those, there is always much to sort out.'

'There is, there is!'

'Business interests, too. Complex ones. That makes it particularly difficult.'

'It does. It does.'

'Especially as he seems to have had business interests everywhere.'

'That is what I keep saying to Juliette. It's not as if his affairs were confined to Tangier, I say.'

'The business trips alone –'

'Exactly! "I have a job," I say to Juliette. "I can't be always going off to places like Marrakesh. I have responsibilities here." But she does not understand!'

'Ah, women!'

'Exactly, Monsieur: women!'

'But perhaps I can help?'

'Help?' said Renaud, disconcerted.

'Over the business trips at least. I have some information on them.'

'You do?'

'Dates, for instance.'

'Dates?'

'And places.'

'Places?'

'And sums. Do you have sums?'

'Well . . .'

'Perhaps we could compare notes. You show me your information and I'll show you mine. I gather you have his papers?'

'Some, yes. Well, most –'

'Then we could go through them together.'

'Um, ah – They are not – not all to hand.'

'You do have them still?'

'Oh, yes. But – some are still to be sorted.'

'We can do that together.'

'Um. Ah. Yes.'

Renaud pulled himself together.

'But before I could do that, I would have to . . . They are Juliette's papers, after all. Private papers. Yes, that's it. Private papers. I feel I ought not to –'

'Naturally, I would not wish to pry into Madame Bossu's private papers. But Bossu's papers . . . Surely Bossu's papers are within the scope of the public investigation?'

'Um. Ah. Yes. But . . .'

Seymour could see that he was not going to let Seymour anywhere near them.

That evening he went to see Monique.

'Well, this is a pleasure,' she said.

Her apartment was tucked away from the sea front but close enough to it and high up enough for him to be able to see the sea. She took him out on to a little balcony which overlooked the bay. It was dark now and the harbour was alive with lights. From the cheap Arab cafés over to their left came the throbbing and wailing of Arab music. They sat down.

'Well, now,' she said, 'I am not so foolish as to imagine that this is just a social call. How can I help you?'

'I am sorry to trouble you over something so small. But I can see no other way of finding out. It is just a very simple question.'

'Simple?' she said. Her eyebrows went up. 'But in Tangier no questions are simple. Because they nearly always lead to difficult answers.'

'This one won't,' said Seymour. 'It is just to ask you if you know the name of the bank Bossu used. And I wouldn't have troubled you if I had been able to get anything sensible out of Juliette.'

'Thousands have tried before you! But I do see that that is the kind of mundane detail that might have escaped her notice.'

'I had hoped, actually, that it might be in Bossu's papers. But Renaud had taken them all away.'

Monique was amused.

'So he's not so stupid!' She thought. 'Actually he's not stupid at all. He can be quite cunning at times. When it's in his interests.'

'So I come to you.'

'It's easy.'

She wrote the name down on a slip of paper. It was the name of the bank in which the committee had its offices.

'That all? Really? Well, I'm not going to let you get away with that. At least you must have a drink.'

Seymour found himself staying rather longer than he had intended.

'So how did you get on with Monique?' asked the receptionist when he came down the next morning.

He stopped.

'You know?'

'Of course.'

'How?'

'Someone saw you. And then came back and told me.'

'Why did they come back and tell you?'

'Cash. I like to know these things.'

'I wouldn't have thought this was worth paying for.'

'I didn't pay very much.'

'Still . . .'

'You have to cast your bread upon the waters if you're a journalist. Usually it leads to nothing. But occasionally there is a return.'

'Is this for your newspaper?'

'My newspaper would certainly pay for information. If it was worth printing.'

'I wouldn't have thought this was.'

'I don't think so, either,' she agreed. 'Still, I didn't know that until after I had paid. It was only a few coins. My informant was a small boy and he brings information rather indiscriminately.'

Seymour laughed.

'Do you use a lot of boys?' he asked.

'I find them useful. And girls, too, but they don't get around so much.'

'Do you know a lame beggar boy?'

'I know several lame beggar boys.'

'Something wrong with his hip.'

She thought for a moment.

'Why do you want to know?'

'Because this one may have seen what happened to Bossu. He was lying in the scrub when Bossu rode in after a pig.'

'It may be Salah,' she said. 'He lives over in that direction and is just the sort of boy who would want to follow the pig-sticking.'

'Where would I find him?'

'You could try the Mosque Al-Baylim. He sleeps there and they give him food.'

'Thank you.'

'If you find out anything,' she said, 'tell me.'

He nodded.

She came to the door with him. As she opened it she saw Mustapha and Idris outside.

'Are they coming with you?'

Seymour sighed.

'Almost certainly.'

'Go easy with them today. It's Ramadan and they don't eat until after sunset. What with that and the heat, people get very exhausted. By the time they'd finished yesterday they were really knocked up.'

'Look, they don't have to come with me.'

'Oh, but they do. It's a question of honour.'

She went across to them and spoke to them. Then she came back.

'I've told them which mosque it is,' she said. 'You'll find Salah asleep in the porch if you go there about noon.'

The Mosque Al-Baylim was on the poor edge of Tangier, where the cheap, flat-roofed houses with tomatoes and onions spread out to dry on the top gave way to the poorer kind of workshops: potteries, consisting of trenches where the potters sat outside on planks and worked their wheels with their bare feet, tanners, where bare-chested men dipped skins into huge vats, underground flour mills in dark cellars where great wheels were driven by subterranean streams, oil presses where the ground around was damp and discoloured and the air was heavy with the sticky, slightly sugary smell of pressed sesame seed.

The mosque itself was next to a tannery and its white stucco walls were stained brown with the effluent. But it was entered through a beautiful, old, wooden porch, all latticework and ornamentation. In the cool of its shade several ragged forms were lying. Mustapha stirred one with his foot.

'Salah?' he said.

Another form sat up.

'Who asks?' it said.

'Mustapha.'

The form scrutinized him carefully.

'I know you,' it said.

'Everybody knows me,' said Mustapha impatiently.

'Why do you want me?' asked the boy in sudden panic.

'I want to talk to you.'

'If it's about that load of kif, I don't know anything about it!'

'It's not about the kif,' said Mustapha, slightly uncomfortably. 'It's about that dead Frenchman. Look, you'd better come out here.'

There was a sudden chorus of protests from the other forms in the porch.

'What are you going to do to him?'

'Leave him alone!'

'He had nothing to do with it!'

'Shut up!' said Mustapha. 'It's not about the kif. I just want to ask him some questions, that's all. About the Frenchman.'

'I've told you everything I know!'

'All I want you to do is tell it once again. Only this time so that my friend will hear.'

'Your friend?'

Salah took in for the first time Seymour's presence.

'Who's he?' he said suspiciously.

'My friend. Like I said. He's an Englishman. From the police in London.'

'The police?'

The porch went still. There was a long silence. Then –

'Mustapha!' the beggar boy said reproachfully.

'What is it?'

'Mustapha, I would never have believed this of you!'

'What are you on about?'

'You, whom I have always heard spoken of as a man of honour!'

'What are you talking about?'

'The police! Mustapha, I would never have believed this of you!'

82

'Have you gone crazy or something!'

'That you, of all men –'

'What's the matter with him?' said Idris.

'It must be big. Of course! I've got it now,' said the beggar boy conciliatorily. 'Really big! Something that will make your fortune. Well, Mustapha, I congratulate you.'

'Either he's mad or I'm mad!' declared Mustapha.

'It's just that I'm – well, surprised, that's all, disappointed. A little.'

'It's him!' said Idris. 'Definitely. He's gone mad.'

'You wouldn't have cut them in on it if it hadn't been really big –'

'What the hell are you talking about?'

'The kif. You wouldn't have sold out to the police if –'

'Shall I just cut his throat?' asked Idris.

There was another chorus from inside the porch.

'Leave him alone!'

'You bastards!'

'Salah,' said Mustapha dangerously, 'I have been very patient with you. But –'

Seymour intervened hastily. He had just about enough Arabic to get it across.

'It's nothing to do with the kif,' he said. 'Mush kif. And there's no deal. Mush deal. I'm interested only in the Frenchman. Tell him that, will you?'

'Mush kif. Mush deal,' said Mustapha. 'Got that, you little bastard? My friend has hit the nail right on the head. And now you're going to tell us, exactly and pretty quickly, just what it was that you saw when that French bastard rode out into the scrub last week.'

'There were two pigs, see. And they ran off to one side. And the fat Frenchman went after them. Then he settled on one and rode after that. I could see him above the scrub, going up and down because the ground rose and fell at that point. And I thought, You'd better watch it, my fat friend, or else you'll come off. And then you'll be in trouble, especially if the pig turns and goes for you. And then I thought, That would be good to see. So I made haste to get there. But, Monsieur, I do not make haste very fast.'

He looked at Seymour apologetically.

'I have to go like this.'

He showed Seymour how he ran: head down, almost touching the ground, hip up higher than his head. It was just like a hyena, Seymour thought.

'And when I raised my head, I could not see him. "Lo, it has happened as I foretold," I said to myself, and redoubled my efforts to get there. I heard the horse in the bushes and ran towards it, but not too fast in case it was the pig and not the horse.

'And then I saw the lance. It was standing upright, just like this. And I thought, That is strange, but it must have fallen so. But when I went closer I saw that it was stuck through the fat Frenchman, and I thought, How can that be? He cannot have fallen thus. And then it came to me that he could not have done it himself and that someone else had a hand in this! So I sat beneath a bush and waited.

'And gradually men came. I heard them speak. "What is this?" they said. "He needs help," someone said. But then someone else said, "Nothing can help him now!" And another said, "Let us not go too close, for the Sheikh will send his men and then it will be better for us if we are not near."

'So they sat down and waited. And then the Sheikh's men came. And they said, "Right, you bastards, who has done this?" And we all said, "Not I!" And they must have believed us, for one stayed and one rode away, and eventually he came back with another Frenchman, the tall captain.

'That is all, and it was thus, and as I told you the first time.'

'Not all,' said Seymour, when Mustapha had finished interpreting.

'Not all?'

'Was not there another horse?'

'Another horse?'

'Didn't someone ride in after the Frenchman? Immediately after.'

'I saw no other horse.'

'Ask him to think again. Carefully. Is he sure there was no other horse?'

Salah shook his head stubbornly.

'I saw no other horse.'

'Think again, Salah, for how else did the lance get there?'

'That's a good one,' said Idris. 'Someone stuck him, didn't they? So someone else must have been there.'

'Ah, but was he on a horse?' asked Mustapha. 'Well, was he, you little bastard?' he said to the beggar boy.

'I saw no one,' repeated the beggar boy. 'And no horse, either.'

'Salah, I believe you,' said Seymour. 'But, then, as my friends say, there is left a riddle. Which, perhaps, you may still help us solve. Go on thinking. Think back to that day. You saw no other horse. Nor person, either. Might that not be because at the time you were running through the scrub with your head down, as you showed me?'

'Well, it might, but –'

'Go on thinking. Salah, you *saw* nothing. But you *heard* something. You told me. Something in the bushes. A pig, you said, or a horse. Could it not have been a horse?'

'Well . . .'

'You, yourself, were in doubt. Now, Salah, you heard this thing in the bushes, and you were concerned lest it might come upon you. Does that mean it was coming towards you? Or was it going away from you?'

'Monsieur, I –'

'Draw it in the sand. With your finger. Here is the spot where the Frenchman fell. And here is the track that he came from, where all the others were. Now, where were you? Draw it.'

Mustapha and Idris bent down to see.

'So, Salah, you were here. Beside the main track?'

'Watching the horses go by, yes.'

'And the Frenchman rode into the scrub here, over to your right hand as you lay?'

'That is so.'

'And disappeared here. And you turned and went up to where you had last seen him. And then you heard something in the bushes . . .?'

'Here,' said Salah, pointing with his finger.

'Near the spot where the fat Frenchman fell, but this side of it. Which means that whoever-it-was was coming away from where he fell?'

'It seems so,' Salah agreed.

'And therefore towards you?'

Salah nodded.

'Now, Salah, think hard. It did not stop, did it, or else you would have seen it when you got near the man. It must have gone on. Now, can you remember: did it pass you, or did it run away over to the left?'

'Monsieur, it was I that ran away.'

'And the horse – or pig?'

'Carried on.'

'Back down to the main track?'

'I think so, Monsieur.'

'Does not that make it seem as if it was a horse?'

'If it was a pig,' said Mustapha, 'it was a very stupid one.'

'But, Monsieur . . .' said Idris.

'Yes?'

'You were asking Salah if there were not two horses. But Salah has been speaking only of one. Might not the horse that passed him have been the fat Frenchman's horse?'

'I didn't hear *two* horses coming towards me,' said Salah. 'That I *do* know.'

Chapter Six

It was now well into the afternoon and the heat, as always in Tangier, had built up. Out in the bay there was a distinct haze. The sea was still, though, and not a boat was moving. Not much was moving on the land, either, and Seymour, mindful of Chantale's injunction, looked around for a place where Mustapha and Idris might take a rest. They were not complaining but their faces were drawn and he guessed that this was the point in the day when they were missing their food.

He suggested that they stop in a café, whose tables conveniently spread out into the road; but when he sat down at a table Mustapha and Idris refused to join him.

'No, no,' they said, 'we'll sit down over here.'

And they sat down across the road in the shade of a big house and rested their backs against the wall.

He tried to persuade them but they were firm.

'No, no: this gives us a better view.'

A better view? An undistinguished street with small, somnolent shops, a dog or two lying in the shade, the shutters on the houses closed and not a sign of life or a thing of interest: except that at the far end of the street there was another café, more populated than this one, with several people sitting at the tables but not much sign of action.

'We can see them if they come,' said Mustapha.

'Both left and right,' said Idris.

If they come? What were they expecting?

He tried again to persuade them but without success. At

least, however, they were sitting down getting some respite, so he decided to leave them alone and ordered himself some mint tea. He wondered if he should order them some, too: but were they allowed to drink during the day? He knew they shouldn't eat during Ramadan, but what about drink?

He went across and put it to them.

They thanked him politely but declined. A sip of water, however, would be welcomed.

Seymour went back to the café and asked if some water could be provided for his friends. He half expected a brusque dismissal, which is what he would certainly have got in England, but instead they nodded approvingly and took some across in an enamel mug; just the one mug, which Mustapha and Idris shared quite happily.

He suddenly realized that he was glad to sit down himself. Although he was in the shade, the heat was still considerable enough to make him languorous. The mint tea, though, was refreshing and he sat on for some time in an increasing doze; which seemed to be shared by everyone around him.

Not at the other end of the street, however. Shouts roused him. People in the café looked up. There seemed to be some sort of altercation centring on the other café. Mustapha, drawn to any form of disorder, went up the street to see what was going on. There was a crowd, growing every second, and voices were raised in protest.

Mustapha returned.

'You'd better come,' he said to Seymour. 'It's Chantale. And the French.'

Seymour rose at once.

'It might be better if it's you,' said Mustapha, 'and not us.'

At the centre of the crowd was a policeman holding a man and beside them was a Frenchwoman, gesticulating fiercely. Beside them, gesticulating just as fiercely, was a fired-up Chantale.

'And take her in, too,' cried the Frenchwoman angrily.

'Yes, take me in, too!' shouted Chantale, equally angry. She held out her wrists as if for handcuffs. 'Take me in! And see what happens!'

'This is injustice!' cried the man the policeman was holding. He was an Arab and seemed to Seymour slightly familiar. Then he worked it out. It was one of the young men, Sadiq's friends, who had been sitting in the café when he had come out of the committee's room with Mr Bahnini.

'He molested me!' cried the Frenchwoman.

'No, he didn't!' shouted Chantale. 'He just sat next to you.'

'I don't want to sit next to a dirty Arab!'

'He doesn't want to sit next to a dirty Frenchwoman!' shouted Chantale wrathfully.

'Hey, hey, hey! You can't say things like that!' said the policeman. Still holding the young man, he made a grab for Chantale.

'Take them both in!' shouted the Frenchwoman furiously. 'Arrest them! He has molested me. And she has insulted me!'

Another policeman appeared. The first policeman handed the man over to him and tightened his grip on Chantale.

'You leave her alone!' shouted someone in the crowd. 'It's Chantale!'

'Hands off, you bastards!' shouted someone else.

'Don't you know how to treat a lady?' cried a third man.

'She's not a lady!' cried the Frenchwoman. 'She's a black!'

The next moment she reeled back from a slap by Chantale.

'Hey, hey, hey!' cried the constable.

'She has insulted us!' cried the young Arab, beside himself. 'Me, Chantale, the whole Moroccan people!'

'Why do we have to put up with this?' called someone from the back of the crowd.

'Yes, why?'

The crowd began to press forward angrily.

The Frenchwoman turned pale.

It was, strictly speaking, no concern of Seymour's. He had no authority here. But old policeman's habits died hard.

He pushed through the crowd.

'Calm yourselves, calm yourselves, Messieurs, Mesdames!'

'I am going to hit her again!' shouted Chantale.

'No, you're not.'

He caught the hand just in time.

Chantale tried to wrench it free, then fell against Seymour. He grabbed her and held on to her.

'Take her to the police station!' cried the Frenchwoman. 'She has assaulted me!'

'Enough!' said Seymour. 'Enough!'

'Enough!' said another voice authoritatively.

A tall man had pushed through the crowd.

'Let go of her!' he said to the policeman holding Chantale. 'And get them away. Quickly!'

'Yes, sir!' said the policeman, releasing Chantale and snapping to attention. 'At once, sir!'

But then he hesitated.

'Which of them, sir?'

'Well . . .'

'She assaulted me!' cried the Frenchwoman.

'She insulted me!' cried Chantale.

'Enough, enough! Madame Poiret, contain yourself! Chantale – really!'

'And he molested me!' said the Frenchwoman, pointing at the young Arab.

'No, I didn't!'

'No, he didn't!' said Chantale.

'No, he didn't,' said the crowd.

'He sat next to her,' said Seymour quietly. 'That appears to be all.'

The man nodded. Seymour recognized him now. It was

the French captain, de Grassac. He recognized Seymour at the same moment.

'Monsieur Seymour!'

'We'd better get them away,' said Seymour.

De Grassac nodded again.

'Follow me,' he ordered the policemen.

He began to push a way through the crowd.

The others followed him, the policemen with their prisoners, Seymour, and Mustapha and Idris.

After they had gone a little way, de Grassac halted.

'Is there really any need to go to the police station?' he asked.

'No,' said Seymour firmly.

'She assaulted me,' said Madame Poiret.

'Perhaps not undeservedly, Madame,' said Seymour.

'She called Chantale a black,' said the young Arab hotly. 'If she had called her a Moroccan, that would have been all right. Chantale would be proud to be called a Moroccan. But to call her a black was an attempt to denigrate.'

'He speaks like a lawyer,' said Madame Poiret.

'I *am* a lawyer,' said the young Arab. 'Or will be one soon.'

'Did you do anything apart from sit next to her?' de Grassac asked.

'No. And I sat next to her because that was the only table free.'

'Is this true, Madame?'

'They should have directed him to another place.'

'Why?' demanded Chantale excitedly. 'Why?'

'Calm down, Chantale. You are not behaving in a seemly way. And nor are you, Madame.'

'I don't believe in letting people get above themselves.'

'Who is this you're talking about?' demanded the young Arab fiercely.

'You,' said Madame Poiret. 'And her,' she said, pointing to Chantale.

'Madame,' said de Grassac, 'Mademoiselle de Lissac is the daughter of a very gallant gentleman with whom I served and I will not allow any aspersion to be made against her honour. Tell your husband that, and tell him that it is Captain de Grassac who says so. If he would like to take it up with me, he knows where to find me.'

'Come, come,' said Seymour. 'There is no need for things to get so far. Captain de Grassac is absolutely right. This is all best forgotten.'

'I am not sure I can let it be forgotten,' said the young Arab stiffly. 'I have been insulted!'

Seymour took him to one side.

'Certainly you have been insulted,' he said. 'And deserve an apology. But I am not sure how much one from this lady would be worth. And there is a complication, which you as a lawyer will certainly appreciate: about the only hard breach of the law that has occurred is that Chantale has struck the lady. Now, do you want her to have to answer for that in a court of law? Or wouldn't you prefer to forget the whole thing?'

The young man hesitated.

'Given the sort of justice we get here,' he said reluctantly, 'it might be best to forget the whole thing. Although when such things happen all the time, it is hard to forget them.'

'Thank you.'

He looked at de Grassac and nodded. De Grassac turned to the two policemen.

'Okay!' he said.

They evidently agreed, for he nodded back.

'Right,' said Seymour, 'off you go!'

The young Arab walked away, with dignity.

'You're not going to let him go?' said Madame Poiret.

'Why not?' said de Grassac. 'He appears to have committed no offence.'

'I shall complain to the Resident-General.'

'Do. And perhaps I will have a word with him myself.

I think, Madame, that it would be best if you went home and sat quietly for a while.'

Madame Poiret paused rebelliously, then shrugged her shoulders and marched off.

The two constables watched her go and then departed, with relief.

'As for you, Chantale –' said de Grassac.

'I am sorry,' said Chantale humbly. 'I should have kept my mouth shut. But when I heard what she was saying to Awad, and saw that the police were going to take him away – it was so unjust!'

'Yes, well, these things happen,' said de Grassac. 'It might be wiser if you didn't get involved so readily.'

'I'm just an unbalanced, emotional Moroccan,' said Chantale, not altogether acquiescently.

'You, Chantale,' said de Grassac, 'are sometimes just a pain in the ass.'

Seymour recalled that he had left his tea abandoned and unpaid for and returned to the café. He invited de Grassac to join him. He also invited Chantale but she declined.

'I have to get back to relieve my mother,' she said. 'Besides, I've caused enough trouble for one day.'

De Grassac watched her go.

'I've known her since she was a child,' he said. 'And sometimes I don't think she's changed a bit.'

'You knew her father, I think you said?'

'De Lissac. We came out to Africa in the same year. We served together. A good man to have beside you. We were very close.'

'You obviously know the family well.'

'Yes. I was the first person he told. When he got married. I warned him. I said, "There will be problems, Marcel!" "So?" he said. "You will help me solve them." And, of course, I said I would. We were comrades. I was the best man at the wedding. Actually, the only other man at the wedding.'

He laughed.

'Of course,' he said, 'they tried to break it up. They posted him all over the place, usually to places she couldn't come to. But, then, to be fair, we were all being posted all over the place, often to places no one had ever heard of, places deep in the Sahara without a name. And I was often posted with him.'

He sipped his tea, and stroked his moustaches.

'In those early years we were always fighting. You really get to know a man when you're under fire together. Especially in tight situations. He saved my life, I saved his. Once we were out on patrol and my horse was hit. It went down and my leg was caught underneath. They were coming in on me and I thought I was done for. But then he came riding back, alone, and pulled me out and up on to his horse, and we rode away together. And once I did the same for him.

'That's when you really get to know a man. And not just then. There were times when we were together at some lonely outpost where nothing happened for weeks, months. You were thrown on each other. It is important then to have good comrades because otherwise you go mad. As some did. You talk, you talk – that is all you can do. And de Lissac and I talked. We put the world right together. For me especially it was an education. I came from a family which didn't talk much, an old army family, you understand? His was like that, too, but he had a grandfather he talked with. About the great things, you know: life, death. And now he talked with me. I had never talked like that before. It was a revelation. So there were these things to life? I had never understood that before.

'And then they had the baby, and we talked about that. Uncomprehending, on my part. I couldn't see why he was so excited. A baby, just a baby, I thought. But now I come to see – I was the godfather. "You ought to get one for yourself," he said, laughing. But I never did. We were always moving, you understand? At the places we were posted to there were never any women of the right sort. So,

94

well, no wife, no baby. The only child I ever held in my arms was his.'

He stroked his moustaches again.

'And then we were posted to Morocco. We even spent some time in Tangier. He was very happy because he could spend time with his wife.'

He looked at Seymour.

'You know Marie? No? A remarkable woman. Stayed with him through thick and thin. And so – so aware of things! At first I was – well, you know, I had my doubts. About her being a Moroccan, you know. But I could see – see she made him happy. And in time I got to know her too. So easy to talk to, so understanding. I forgot she was Moroccan. What did I care about that sort of thing? What did it matter if she was brown, black, pink or whatever? She was the wife of a brother officer. That was enough.'

He stopped.

'And then we were sent to Casablanca.'

He hesitated.

'You know about Casablanca.'

'A little.'

'Yes. Well. There you are.'

He studied his cup, and was silent for quite some time. Then he looked up.

'It made a difference. Everything in Morocco today, you know, goes back to Casablanca. For good or bad. And I'm not saying it was all for the bad. But it changed everything. And it changed everything for him, too.

'We were sent to Casablanca. It was just another place, one of the many we had been sent to. But for de Lissac it was not just another place. It was different because of what we had to do there.

'And perhaps de Lissac himself had become different by this time. Perhaps it was the child, I don't know. Or per-haps it was that we were now in Morocco and his wife was Moroccan. He began to think, and to think differently from the rest of us. He had always thought differently. I realize that now, but now his thinking was taking him apart from us.

'After his first day in Casablanca he said, "This is not right." And after his second he said, "I am not going to do this."

'Well, it was a bad time to make his stand. They had began to fight back and we ourselves were under fire. At such times, you understand, you stand together. So, many were angry with him. I was angry with him. Our Commandant pulled him out. "We'll sort this out later," he said. "This is not the time."

'But for de Lissac it *was* the time. If no one does anything now, he said, no one ever will! So he began to show himself and speak and people began to notice him. "You see?" said the Moroccans. "Even the army is beginning to question!"

'And the townspeople, the interests, the big interests, yes? became angry. What are you doing? they said. Whose side are you on? He's stirring up trouble. He's making things worse.

'Our Commandant didn't know what to do. He told Marcel to shut up. But Marcel said it was a matter of principle and that he wouldn't shut up. In that case, said the Commandant, you'd better resign. Very well, then, said Marcel. I *will* resign. And he did.

'But then he still didn't shut up. He went on protesting. "You've got to do something about this!" the townspeople said. "What can I do?" said the Commandant. "He's not in the army now." "That's not stopping you doing things to everyone else," they said. "Get rid of him!" And in the end he had to. We hustled him away. Locked him up. It was the sort of thing you could do then. No one was asking any questions. Certainly not in Casablanca. And not in Tangier, either.

'Well, we afterwards lost touch. The regiment was posted. And then we heard that he had died. Well, of course, I wrote to Marie. But we were a long way away. I did wonder how they were getting on, but . . .

96

'Then, one day, we were posted back to Tangier, and I went to see them. And what I found made me go straight to the General. "General," I said, "we've got to do something! He was a good man, a good officer, too. And one of us. We can't just leave them. And there's his daughter, too. Damn it, she's half French. You can't just leave her in this sort of state." I told the others, too, and in the mess things got quite heated. They sent a deputation in support of me. "You've got to do something," they told the General. And, to be fair, he did.

'But, you know, when things happen like what happened just now, I wonder if we got it right. But perhaps you can never get these things right . . .'

'My thoughts,' confessed Mustapha, behind him, 'are not always godly.'

'No?'

'Sometimes I think about food.'

'Well, Mustapha, that is understandable. Especially at Ramadan time.'

'Ramadan will soon be over, God be praised. No, I don't mean that! I mean, Ramadan will soon be over.'

'That is so, Mustapha. And then we will be able to return to ungodly things.'

'That will be needful, Idris. For by then the money will have run out.'

Mustapha was silent for a moment. Then he said: 'Idris?'

'Yes, Mustapha?'

'Do you think God sees into the heart?'

'He does, Mustapha.'

'He will know, then, that instead of thinking holy thoughts, I think about food?'

'I am afraid so, Mustapha.'

'And that I said I was looking forward to the end of Ramadan?'

'God knows everything.'

'It's a bad lookout, Idris.'

97

Idris, too, was silent for a moment, reflecting.

'On the other hand,' he said, 'there are things that will count for you. You have, after all, been observing Ramadan, and that surely must count for something.'

'Well, that is true, Idris,' said Mustapha, relieved.

'And then, since our friend arrived and we have been looking after him, we have not actually been doing things that we ought not to have been doing.'

'That also is true, Idris. And it is bound to come on the credit side.'

'The credit side may even outweigh the debit side by now.'

'God be praised!' said Mustapha, relieved.

'Besides, God sees all and knows all. He knows that we are frail.'

'Bound to,' agreed Mustapha.

'And makes allowances.'

'God be praised!'

Silence.

'Idris?'

'Yes, Mustapha?'

'He's going to have to make a lot of allowance in my case.'

When they got back to the hotel Seymour assured Mustapha and Idris that he could now safely be left to his own devices.

'That's what you think,' said Mustapha.

'Look, I'll be all right. I'm used to handling things on my own. In England –'

'Ah, in England!' said Mustapha sceptically.

'I am a policeman, after all!'

Mustapha said nothing, but exuded doubt.

'Anyway, who is going to attack me? I won't go anywhere daft, I promise you. And there isn't anyone out looking for me.'

'No?' said Mustapha and Idris, together.

'No. No one in Tangier has even heard of me.'

Mustapha and Idris said nothing.

'Well, have they?' he demanded.

'Not *heard* of you exactly,' said Mustapha.

'But seen you,' said Idris. 'And once seen, not forgotten. They'll want to pay you back.'

'Pay me back? But I haven't done anything to be paid back for!'

'No?'

'Look, stop being so mysterious and tell me what this is all about. To the best of my knowledge I've not offended anybody since I arrived in Tangier!'

'Just think,' said Idris.

'The first night,' said Mustapha.

'The first night?' said Seymour. 'Nothing happened the first night.'

'Was helping me nothing?' asked Mustapha.

'Helping – you don't mean that bunch could have it in for me?'

'Things like that are not forgotten.'

'That's ridiculous!'

'Maybe, but we'll stick around. We know Ali Khadr and his boys.'

In the end he half persuaded them. Mustapha went home to his evening meal while Idris nobly accompanied Seymour to his.

He passed a little French restaurant and saw Monsieur L'Espinasse sitting inside at the window. He was dining alone and his face brightened when he saw Seymour.

'No, no. Please. It will be a pleasure.'

So Seymour, another single man, joined him at the table and benefited from the Secretary's deep knowledge of the dishes.

'Some say it is the sauce,' said L'Espinasse, 'and some say the care with which Vincent chooses the raw materials.

It is all those things but as well he has a certain – touch. Yes? A flair. I have always found him very reliable.'

From one reliable French topic to another, and soon they turned to a different French passion, *la chasse*. There was, said the Secretary, a natural affinity between the French and hunting. So it was not surprising how the new people took to it when they came out here. Of course, wild boars had been hunted in France since the Middle Ages and the pursuit was still practised in many parts of the country. But not quite like this: the mad (the word which suggested itself most readily to Seymour) chase on horseback armed only with a lance. And the boars, like the Moroccans, were wilder. But this, concluded the Secretary, gave only the more opportunity for the expression of French élan.

'Yes, indeed!' said Seymour enthusiastically. It was wonderful to see the true French spirit carried across the sea in this way. And unfortunate that the Moroccans, with the exception of Sheikh Musa, did not appear to have taken it up with the zest of the French. But that was probably because they lacked that natural affinity the Secretary had spoken of.

From what he had seen, however, there was no shortage of devotees in Tangier. He asked what sort of backgrounds they came from.

'The members, you mean? Mostly settlers. People on the farms locally, although some come from quite a distance, fifty kilometres or more. The farms are all in the coastal strip. It's not very deep, twenty kilometres at most, but, of course, it goes right along the coast. It includes what will be the Spanish Zone under the new treaty, and that is a source of worry to some of the settlers. I mean, they're French, not Spanish. But will they still be eligible for the pig-sticking? That's important because it gets them off the farm for a bit and they can forget for a while how much money they're not making. I speak from experience. I'm a settler myself.

'And then there are the soldiers, of course. There's usually a big contingent of those. I would say they're the keenest members. Goes with the job, I suppose. If you're cavalry, and a lot of them are. And then, of course, they've the time to practise. Some of them are really rather good.'

'Businessmen?' asked Seymour.

'A few. Like Bossu. But not many. They're all too busy making money. More, people in professional jobs, doctors, lawyers, that sort of thing. Like Meunier and Millet. Though those two don't actually hunt.'

'*Fonctionnaires?*'

Officials? There weren't many of those at the moment, although doubtless that would change when the Protectorate was more established. At the moment most officials, in fact practically all of them, except when they were French army officers, were Moroccan and worked in the old Ministries under the Mahzen.

'Under the shade of the Parasol,' said L'Espinasse with a smile, 'where they can doze in peace.' No, they weren't much interested.

'Not even in Musa's old Ministry?'

'The Ministry of War? No, they're either old soldiers like Musa but who believe in killing people not pigs; or young men who are interested only in the latest armaments and pooh-pooh the whole idea of pig-sticking. And, besides . . .'

'Yes?'

The Secretary frowned.

'There is a question about them; how far are they really committed to the Protectorate? Some of them are – well, a little difficult. A little too political, if you know what I mean. They have ideas – ideas which are not always ours. They keep their distance. Well, I can understand that. But it is unfortunate because we don't develop a shared – well, I don't know what it is we share, but it is something. Or could be. No, it's rather sad that the young keep their distance. And, of course, that means that they don't become members of the hunt.'

'So all French, then?'

101

'Nearly all. Except, of course, Musa and one or two of his friends.'

Most interesting. Seymour would not be here long but he would like to get to know people. The members of the hunt, for instance. They seemed a nice bunch. Monsieur L'Espinasse had spoken of affinity and he, Seymour, certainly felt . . .

He wondered if the Secretary could even let him have a list of members. Monsieur L'Espinasse certainly could. In fact, he had in his pocket at this very moment the membership booklet and if Monsieur would like . . .

Chapter Seven

The bank was a modern one, European in style, with glassed-in counters and besuited men all over the place. Not entirely European, though: the men were wearing fezzes and great fans were whirring overhead. The manager was Moroccan but you would have taken him for French. He spoke French naturally and fluently and looked French with his natty dark suit and carefully cut hair. He had Macfarlane's letter of introduction on the desk in front of him.

'Monsieur Seymour?' They shook hands. 'And what can I do for you?'

Seymour explained why he was in Tangier and said that the investigation was of some importance to the international community and in particular the international financial community and that he hoped therefore that the bank would be able to help him. The manager said that it certainly would.

'We knew Bossu, of course.'

'I gather he banked with you?'

'That is true, yes.'

Seymour put a piece of paper in front of him.

'I wonder if you would mind checking if these sums were paid from his account?'

The manager summoned a minion and gave the paper to him. The man went off.

'They may well not have been,' said Seymour, 'since I think it quite likely that the payments were made to people in the interior.'

'I doubt if they would have been made by cheque then. Unless the cheques were going to be brought back here. There are no banks in the south and I doubt if the moneylenders down there would accept cheques.'

'That is what I thought. I gather that in the interior payment is usually made in hard form.'

'They even still use Maria Theresa dollars!'

'So even if he had originally drawn the money from here, he would probably have changed it into coin or bullion?'

'Very probably.'

'I wonder if you could tell me how he would go about doing that?'

'He would probably have gone to one of the big moneylenders in the medina.'

Monsieur Seymour must understand that the Moroccan economy was, well, a mixed one, a mixture of old and new. Many people, particularly those in the countryside, preferred the traditional ways and still went to the moneylender in the souk rather than to a modern bank. And in some ways that suited the banks. They didn't want to be bothered with handing out often small sums to people they didn't know and – probably wisely – didn't trust. Whereas the moneylenders had their own contacts and so their own ways of assessing creditworthiness. They were used to such transactions and kept their own reserves of hard form money. So if you were planning a business venture to the interior, say, to buy salt, the moneylender was the man to go to.

And did the manager have any idea of the moneylender that Monsieur Bossu might have gone to?

The manager thought. The sums Monsieur Seymour had mentioned were quite large so it would have been one of the big ones. He would give Monsieur Seymour three names . . .

The minion returned. There was no record, he said, of the sums mentioned being paid from Monsieur Bossu's account. In any case, the balance in Monsieur Bossu's account would have been far too small.

In the medina, like businesses were gathered together. Here, for example, was the leather-making quarter, consisting of little box-like shops where the proprietor sat on the usual counter with his wares spread around him. Behind him in dark inner rooms squatting figures traced intricate designs on saddles and bags and slippers, and the strong smell of leather spread out into the street. Here, now, were the copper workers and from inside came the sounds of hammering and beating and sometimes the hot breath of a fire. And here were the herbalists, their shops heralded by subtle and pungent odours, and often with huge pyramids of fresh green mint on the ground outside.

So it was no surprise to find the moneylenders grouped together, too. No counters in the shops here. Customers sat against the walls, on worn leather cushions if it looked as if their business might be worth it, and in the space in the middle were sets of scales. Some were small and into their cups coins were counted out in two and threes. Others were large and into their bowls were put heavy bags. The bags were always opened before being weighed and often borrowers would thrust their hands in and feel deep. Everything had to be seen; if possible, touched.

Mustapha and Idris, listless from their Ramadan fasting, brightened up when they came to the Street of the Moneylenders. The sight of the coins had a stimulating effect on them and they were inclined to linger outside the shops, looking in, drooling.

'All right for some,' said Idris wistfully.

They stopped outside a small, exceptionally dirty shop.

'This is the one to go to!' they said firmly.

'No, I don't think so,' said Seymour.

'Babikar's all right!' they insisted.

'No, I want a big one.'

'It'll cost you!' they warned.

'I want –' he consulted the list the bank manager had given him – 'Mohammed Noor.'

'Mohammed Noor!' They reeled back. 'Well, if you say so . . .'

They found the shop and went in. Mohammed Noor, seeing a European and deducing therefore that he was wealthy, came forward. Mustapha and Idris slipped back against the wall.

'I come on behalf of a friend,' said Seymour.

'Of course!' said Mohammed smoothly, and clapped his hands.

An attendant brought tea.

None was offered to Mustapha and Idris. However, their presence was accepted; as if the kind of people Mohammed Noor sometimes dealt with were the kind of people who naturally brought their own bodyguards.

Mohammed Noor did not force the pace. They talked of this and that, how long Seymour had been in the country, how he found Tangier. The moneylender spoke French, with the same fluency and ease as the bank manager and, indeed, many of the Moroccans Seymour had met. It transpired, from something he said to Idris, that he also spoke Berber; and, probably, English and Italian and Senussi and a dozen other languages as well.

Gradually they got round to business. Seymour explained that he was acting on behalf of a friend who wanted to make a trading expedition into the interior. The price of salt was rising in Algeria and his friend wished to buy a lot of it; for that, of course, he would need a lot of money, and in appropriate form. Might Mohammed Noor be able to accommodate him?

Mohammed Noor, who, of course, believed none of it, spread his hands and said that nothing could be easier.

Seymour named a sum. Mustapha and Idris, who might have fallen over if the wall had not been behind them, gasped. Mohammed Noor did not turn a hair.

There would be no difficulty, he said.

And what might be the interest charged, asked Seymour.

This time it was Seymour who gasped.

Mohammed Noor spread his hands apologetically.

Of course, he didn't like to impose such charges, he said, and normally wouldn't. But things were deteriorating in the interior, there were rumours of war. The local tribes were unreliable, there were bandits . . .

He could come down just a little, perhaps, in view of the extra security that someone like a friend of Monsieur Seymour would be able, he was sure, to offer. But . . .

And so it went on. And on. In the end Seymour said he would have to consult his friend.

Mohammed Noor, who had not expected otherwise, smiled and said he was always there.

As they were going out, Seymour said that Mohammed Noor's name had been mentioned to him by an acquaintance, a Frenchman, a Monsieur Bossu, who had himself made use of Mohammed's services not long ago. Did Mohammed Noor recall him, he wondered?

Mohammed Noor pondered, but shook his head.

And Seymour moved on to the next one.

Mustapha and Idris had cottoned on by this time and restrained their gasps, although they continued to look slightly alarmed. Even the distant contemplation of such sums disturbed them.

The third moneylender they went to was Abdulla Latif. By this time Seymour had drunk so much mint tea that he was feeling a strain on the system. Abdulla Latif was as prepared to be obliging as the others; so much so that Seymour asked a supplementary question, whether by chance Abdulla knew of any sturdy men who might be willing to accompany his friend into the south. Abdulla Latif said that there were always such men around but that he could supply Seymour with some names if he wished.

As they left, Seymour stopped and turned. Did Abdulla Latif by any chance recall a Frenchman . . .?

Abdulla Latif frowned and then said he thought he did. Seymour said that in matters of this sort it was as well to go by recommendation and his acquaintance – a Monsieur Bossu, was it? – had spoken highly of Abdulla's services. Abdulla bowed and said that he recalled his client perfectly. He had been able to be of use to him on several occasions.

'Twenty per cent!' said Mustapha, as they walked away. 'Twenty per cent!'

Seymour thought he was registering the enormity of the charge. But he wasn't.

'See, that's what those big blokes can get away with. Someone like our friend can go in and they're all over him. "It's just twenty per cent for you, sir." Whereas it's bloody forty per cent for someone like you or me, Idris!'

'What was that about a bodyguard?' asked Idris. 'Your friend's not planning a trip down south, is he? Because if he is, we could fix him up.'

'No, no. There isn't any friend. It was just a trick to get the information out of him.'

'Pity!' said Idris.

'The journey's already been made,' said Seymour. 'By Bossu.'

And then –

'Just a minute!' he said. 'Do you do this sort of thing? Sometimes?'

'If the money's right, yes. Why not?'

'Down south?'

'Well, probably not far. We're city people, really.'

'You didn't, by any chance, go down with someone to Azrou and Immauzer?'

'No, no. Miles away.'

'Too hot!'

'Bloody camels!'

'Not our sort of thing.'

'We have been down occasionally, of course. But that would have been on a run.'

'And in a truck. I mean, camels!'

'Okay, not you, then. But you know people who do that sort of thing? Act as a bodyguard?'

'Oh, sure,' said Mustapha casually.

'Listen, do you know anyone who's made a trip down to those places? Azrou and Immauzer? And Tafilalet?'

'Don't think so. Could ask around, I suppose.'

'Would you? It would have been several months ago. I've got the dates here. A Frenchman. Carrying money. Quite a lot. Probably would have paid well.'

'Sounds interesting,' said Idris.

'It was bad,' said Chantale, cast down. 'It was bad.'

And it was bound to get back to her mother.

Seymour was amused. Here was this woman, who seemed so supremely competent, informed, it appeared, on just about everything. On good terms with all and sundry, able to fix practically anything – and alarmed, like a schoolgirl, that her mother might hear of her transgressions!

'Your mother?'

'It was in the quarter,' said Chantale gloomily. 'You don't know our quarter. And you don't know my mother. Everything in the quarter gets back to her sooner or later.'

'And that matters?'

'It does. Apart from everything else it is an offence against the *caida*. You know about the *caida*? No? Well, you ought to, because it runs through and affects everything you do in Morocco. It is – well, I suppose the French word for it is etiquette. But it is more than that. It is a sort of web which touches everything. It enters into all a Moroccan does . . . into the way you conduct yourself to others. Not just politeness but tact, sensitivity, respect. And I'm pretty certain that my mother's not going to feel I showed a lot of that towards Madame Poiret.'

'She asked for it!'

'No, no, that's a Western thing to say. It's too brusque, harsh. It sounds aggressive. And that's part of the problem for Westerners. Whenever they speak, it sounds wrong. It sounds like that. We Westerners –' She caught herself and laughed. 'We. Me! In our clumsy way we are always offending against the *caida*. And when we do, the Moroccan shrinks back. He withdraws. And so the West never quite meets the East. They never quite come into contact. The Moroccans are terribly polite to them but somehow there is no engagement. You have to be sensitive to the requirements of the *caida* or else you can never really quite speak to a Moroccan.

'And, of course, if you are a Moroccan, it's worse. My mother will be shocked and hurt at what I've done. She will say that I've put her to shame – that everyone will say she's not brought me up properly. She will think I've let her down.'

'Oh, come on! My impression was that everyone in the crowd agreed with you.'

But Chantale was not convinced.

'She will feel that even if Madame Poiret was in the wrong, I still ought not to have struck her. She will think it lowering on my part. A lapse of standards. You have to behave properly even to people who don't behave properly to you. It's a question of – well, I suppose it's like *noblesse oblige*. If you're part of the *caida*, you're like *noblesse*. That's the way I ought to think and behave and if I don't, she will feel she has failed.'

'But, look –'

Chantale shook her head.

'You don't know what it means to my mother. She has struggled to bring me up. And most of the time on her own. And part of that is being true to the way a well-bred Moroccan should behave. The Moroccan bit is important. She doesn't want me to lose touch with – well, the Moroccan side of me. And now look what I've done!'

She looked at him tragically with her large, tear-stained eyes and Seymour found his knees turning to jelly.

'Put it down to the French side of you!' he said, in an attempt to lighten things.

She shook her head again.

'She wouldn't like that *either*. She also wants me to be true to my father. And to that side, the French side, as well. She has rather an idealized picture of that, too. He always had such beautiful manners. I mean, to everyone, high or low, the meanest beggar. He always treated them with respect. You could feel it when he spoke to anyone. It was a bit like the *caida*. Or that's how she would understand it. So she would feel I've let her down on that, too.'

He could see that it was very important to her and that an attempt to jolly her would be wrong.

'You're caught between both sides, I see that,' he said. 'And perhaps between unrealistic expectations on both sides?'

She shook her head fiercely.

'No!' she said. 'Don't say that! She is right. I must be true to both sides of me. The *best* of both sides. That was what my father would have wanted. My mother knows that. And she has tried to bring me up to be like that. Only, sometimes – sometimes it's not easy.'

'I think you're terrific,' said Seymour. 'And I think it's a terrific ideal. And I'm not surprised if you can't always live up to it.'

He heard a door close somewhere nearby in the house behind the counter and wondered if someone was coming.

'Look,' he said, 'why don't I take you out to dinner? Or would that be another Western breach of *caida*?'

She sat back, as if slightly shocked.

Then she smiled.

'No decent Moroccan girl would allow herself to be seen out at night alone with a man. Even in a restaurant. However –' she pretended to consider – 'a French one would,

I suppose. Think of me, for the purposes of this evening, as French. I will ask my mother to cover the desk.'

She suggested a place near the Kasbah and a little later they were making their way through some of the streets he'd passed through earlier. Then they had struck him as seedy. Now, however, the darkness concealed the grime and dilapidation and the moonlight picked out things he'd not previously noticed; carved doorways, ornamental arches, delicate columns.

They went through one of the arches into a small patio with a fountain and trees. One of the trees must have been an orange tree for they suddenly walked into a heavy waft of orange blossom. A spiral staircase wound up out of the patio and they found themselves on an upper balcony on which men were sitting on leather cushions around low tables.

They chose a table at one end of the balcony, from which they could look down on to the patio. The evening was heavily warm but the fountain freshened the air. A waiter brought small bowls of olives and nuts and little plates of salted cakes.

Chantale hesitated.

'They do serve alcohol,' she said, 'but perhaps that had better wait until the meat.'

Instead, they drank fruit juice, freshly made and deliciously cool.

'It's what most Moroccans stick to,' she said. 'But the French – and a lot of French come here – can't get through a whole evening without wine.'

'This is a Moroccan evening, is it?' he said.

'Do you mind?'

'Not at all. I find it . . .' He searched for the word and found that only the French one would do. '. . . *sympathique.*'

She seemed pleased.

'Yes,' she said. 'That is the right thing to feel.'

Everything was relaxed, soft, gentle. The voices were low and courteous. There was no loud laughter as there probably would have been in England. The people smiled and touched each other affectionately, intimate but without any sexual connotations, simply enjoying the social contact. This was Arab, he thought, at its best.

Yes, *sympathique* was the word. But it was an odd one to use after the way he had been spending his time. It wasn't his preoccupation with Bossu but everywhere he had had the sense of strain, of tension barely contained. It had been there on the street that first night when he had intervened on behalf of Mustapha, there in the pig-sticking and in the presence of the soldiers, everywhere. There, too, in people's conversations: in the conversation with Sadiq and Mr Bahnini, and with the Resident-General and Mr Suleiman, with Juliette and with Monique, running all the time like an undercurrent.

He said this to Chantale and she nodded.

'Yes,' she said, 'that is Morocco, too.'

She was the only woman on the balcony. He wondered if that, too, was Morocco.

It didn't seem to bother Chantale. But was there a hint of defiance in her assurance? A deliberate, un-Moroccan assertiveness? He wouldn't put it past her. But if there was, it co-existed with the lack of assertiveness that he had found before in Arab women. Or was that just a question of manners, something shared with the men, a quintessential difference from Western culture?

Later, they went up another flight of stairs to another balcony, where again people were sitting at low tables and where the ripple of the fountain was even more gentle, but where they had the compensation of being more exposed to the moon so that the whole balcony was bathed in its soft light.

Some of the people up there were clearly French, and there were women among them. So far as he could see there was no sense of strain.

Waiters brought silver bowls, towels and kettles of cold

113

water so that they could rinse their hands before eating. That, said Chantale, was absolutely required because the food was eaten with the fingers only and also because the polite thing to do was pluck out tasty morsels from the dish in front of you and offer them to your neighbour.

She reached out a hand, took up some couscous, moulded it with her fingers into a little ball and placed it on Seymour's plate.

'Bismillah,' she said. 'That means: In the name of God. But it is not just religious, it is part of the *caida*. It makes the food more than just food. Not exactly holy, but special.'

Later when the main dish came, a kind of pastrilla, with layers of different meats underneath a crust of delicious flaky pastry, he reached into the dish, took out some pigeon, and put it on her plate.

'*Bismillah*,' he said.

Sitting at the receptionist's desk when they returned to the hotel was a middle-aged Moroccan lady.

'My mother,' said Chantale.

She smiled at Seymour and there was something in her smile that reminded him of her daughter. She was still a beautiful woman but the face was thin and drawn, as if it had seen harsh times, and the large, dark eyes were wary. They appraised Seymour in much the same way, he thought, as his own mother's eyes appraised any woman he brought home for the evening. He thought he would say this to Chantale later. It might comfort her.

'One of the pleasures of Tangier, Madame,' he said, 'has been meeting your daughter.'

'Tangier has many pleasures,' she said neutrally.

Just at that moment the front door of the hotel opened and Mustapha came in.

He stopped when he saw Chantale's mother.

'Madame!' he said.

'Why, Mustapha!' said Chantale's mother, with unaffected pleasure. 'How are you keeping? And your wife?'

'Well, Madame.'

'And the child?'

'Well, too, Madame. He has had chickenpox.'

'But better now, I hope?'

'Oh, yes, he has put it behind him. Another one is on the way.'

'Another child? Oh, how nice for you both! Congratulations, Mustapha! And to your wife as well.'

She suddenly looked anxious.

'Mustapha . . .'

'Madame?'

'Which midwife are you going to use?'

'Maryam, we thought.'

Chantale's mother pursed her lips.

'Maryam is getting old now, Mustapha. And your wife had difficulties the last time.'

'I know, but –'

'Why not try Aisha?'

'Well . . .'

'If it's money, Mustapha, we can help.'

'It's not money, Madame. Though thank you very much. It's . . .' He twisted awkwardly. 'Well, the fact is, we had a little to-do with her husband a few weeks ago and he got hurt. Not badly, not badly,' he hastened to add. 'But things have not been the same between the families since, and I don't like to ask her.'

'But this is ridiculous! She's very fond of you all, and, you know, these days, Mustapha, she would be a much better bet. You want the child to be all right, don't you?'

'Oh, Madame!'

'Of course, you do. And you want your wife to be all right, too. You mustn't let these foolish quarrels get in your way. Aisha would be much the safest choice.'

'Yes, Madame. I know. But . . .'

'But what, Mustapha?'

Mustapha hesitated.

'I – I don't like to go, Madame.'

'Mustapha!'

'Madame?'

'Mustapha, you're not scared, are you?'

'Scared? Me?'

'No, no, of course you're not scared. I didn't mean that. I meant that – it's not easy for you to climb down, is it?'

'Well, no, Madame. Not with Hussein.'

'Would you like me to have a word with Aisha?'

Mustapha crossed the foyer and then, with unexpected grace, kissed her hand.

'I will speak to her tomorrow.'

'Mustapha,' said Chantale, 'did you come in for something?'

'Well, yes, Chantale, as a matter of fact I did. It's like this. We've heard that Ali Khadr and some of his boys are coming over tomorrow night and, knowing how you feel about these things, we wanted to tell you ahead. Knowing how you feel about these things.'

'There is to be no fighting,' said Chantale peremptorily.

'No, no, there won't be. It's just a case of getting a few of our lads together to defend ourselves.'

'No fighting!'

'Yes, but they're coming over. And we can't just stand there, can we? I mean, it would look bad, wouldn't it?'

'Where does Ali Khadr come from, Mustapha?' asked Chantale's mother.

'The Sukhariya.'

'Oh, I know that part. Why don't I go over and talk to him?'

'Oh, no, no!' said Mustapha, appalled. 'You can't do that!'

'Oh, yes, I can. I know that part. I used to go to the mosque there. I know, why don't I go to the mosque? They'll soon put a stop to it.'

'No, no, really. Madame! Really! It's just a bit of harmless fun. We don't want to get the mosque mixed up in this. I don't think religion and – well, not religion – ought to mix.'

'I'll go this evening,' said Chantale's mother with decision. 'After seeing Aisha.'

Mustapha left, unhappy. In the moment before the door closed Seymour heard Idris's voice.

'Well, you really mucked that up, didn't you?'

Chapter Eight

The next morning Seymour went to see Mr Bahnini. He showed him the membership list of the hunt that Monsieur L'Espinasse had given him.

'Do you know any of these men?'

Mr Bahnini studied the list.

'I know quite a few of them.'

'Did any of them use to come here? To see Bossu?'

'One or two, yes.'

He gave Seymour their names.

'Do you know what they wanted to see him about?'

'They probably wished to make some representation. On a point of interest concerning their business usually.'

'Can you tell me what their business was?'

Mr Bahnini looked at the names again.

'Something to do with the railway. They all work for contracting firms.'

'In Tangier?'

'All over the place.'

'In Casablanca?'

'Certainly.'

'Wasn't there some question of a railway in Casablanca? A few years ago?'

'It was just a local railway. Connecting a quarry with a building project on the sea front.'

'And were these men by any chance something to do with that?'

'Yes. Yes, I think they were. I remember their names. I did some of the contracts. I had just started working

118

for Monsieur Bossu at the time and remember being surprised.'

'Surprised?'

'At how big they were. In relation to the project, the railway, that is, for it was just a small one. But I think the contracts took in a number of other things as well.'

'There was nothing odd about them?'

'No, no. People raised questions about them at the time but they always do. In my experience ordinary people don't understand contracts. Because they don't understand them, and because they're suspicious of lawyers, they think they're all part of some conspiracy by the rich. But usually they're just straightforward arrangements for the conduct of business. The rich like to tie things down in case they lose money.'

'And you were working at the time for Monsieur Bossu?'

'Yes, he had lured me out of the Ministry.'

'Which Ministry was that?'

'The Ministry of War.'

'Under Sheikh Musa, would that have been?'

'A long way under. I was in the Accounts section. That was, actually, quite a good place to be in Morocco. You were safe there. Under the Parasol. No one could get at you. And under Musa you weren't asked to do wrong things. They gave you a good training, too. It was always easy to get a good job after you'd worked for them. That may have been why Monsieur Bossu wanted me. If ever a man needed a good accountant, he did.'

'Because he was often doing things that were questionable?'

Mr Bahnini considered.

'Perhaps a little,' he conceded. 'They seemed so to me. We would never have done them in the Ministry. But, I thought, maybe that was the way things were done in business? But I wouldn't say they were ever more than questionable. Not downright dishonest.'

He smiled.

119

'That wasn't the way he made his money, if that was what you were thinking. He earned it through fees, usually for negotiating something. He was very good at that.'

'And this railway that you mentioned, did he have a hand in negotiating that?'

'Yes. It was one of his earlier jobs. And I don't think he did it very well, not as well as he would have done later. The route of the railway led through a Muslim cemetery and that caused all sorts of trouble. People said afterwards that he ought to have foreseen it and bought them off.'

'It was thought to have sparked off the trouble, I gather?'

'Well, yes.'

'There was a lot of feeling about it?'

'Oh, there was. Even in my own family. Sadiq was very difficult at the time. He was still at school and the students got very worked up about it. For weeks he wouldn't even speak to me. It was a relief when he went away to university. The strain on my wife . . .! So when Monsieur Bossu moved back to Tangier and asked me to go with him I was only too glad to go.

'Of course, you never escape from these things. Afterwards I was always known as Bossu's man. So you can understand that when he died, I was – well, I won't say pleased, that would be a nasty thing to say, and he had always treated me fairly, but – I felt as if a load had been lifted off me. I saw a chance to start again. I could even go back to Casablanca, which is where I came from originally, although it would not be easy.

'That is why, when Mr Macfarlane asked me to stay on, I refused. I just couldn't. I feel that I couldn't, any longer.'

When he went out, the group of young men were sitting again in the café across the street. He could see Sadiq, and also the other one, who had been involved in the altercation with Chantale the day before, Awad. When they saw him, Awad said something to Sadiq and they both jumped up and came across to him.

'I would like to express my thanks for your intervention yesterday, Monsieur. At the time I wasn't sure whether I should accept your suggestion – I wanted to make a stand! But, on reflection, I see that you were right.'

Seymour said that was very generous of him, and that he had been talking to Chantale, and that she was taking more or less the same line. It ended with Awad and Sadiq inviting him across the road to join the group at the table.

They were mostly drinking tea, although some were having fruit juice. At first they were rather shy but then, led by Awad and Sadiq, they began to question him eagerly: about England, certainly, but also about Istanbul. They were all radical but also, it seemed to him, very naive. They took as their pattern the recent revolution in Istanbul which had led to the ousting of the Sultan. It was what they had hoped for in Morocco: but then the French had stepped in!

What, now, in the new circumstances, should they do? Leave the country or stand up for a new Morocco here? He had the feeling that it was something they discussed endlessly. Probably it was what they spent their days doing.

Exile or resolution? Twist, or bust? He could see it was a very exciting thing to discuss. But would it ever issue in anything? Would it stay at just talk?

Or not?

Another conversation was going on, apparently endlessly, behind him.

'Mustapha, I told you it was a mistake to warn Chantale!'

'Well, I had to, didn't I? After what happened that other time.'

'Yes, but we'll be over there this time.'

'She still won't like it.'

There was a pause. Then Idris said: 'Suppose we hit them at their place? Before they've even started?'

'We could do that,' Mustapha conceded.

'Well, then . . .'

'But it would make no difference. If she's already been to the mosque.'

'Maybe it wouldn't.' It was Idris who conceded this time. 'But I still don't like it!' he said.

'Well, I don't, either.'

'They've got to be taught a lesson. That's what I said, Mustapha, if you remember. That's what I said to you at the time. "They've got to be taught a lesson." There are rules in this game and they've got to follow them. Otherwise, things get bloody lawless!'

'I was waiting, Idris.'

'We shouldn't have waited. We should have hit them hard straightaway. Because if we don't, they'll do it again.'

'I hear what you are saying, Idris.'

'It's our territory, isn't it? And they invaded it. Came right in. If we let them get away with it, they'll be over here again. And again. And then it won't be our territory any more, will it? It'll be theirs!'

'I know exactly what you mean, Idris.'

'Well, then . . .'

'I was waiting. Shall I tell you why? Because I wanted to find out who was behind it. Look, I know Ali Khadr. He wouldn't have done this on his own. It would never have entered his thick head. Someone must have put him up to it. Put him up to it, and maybe even paid him a bit, because he wouldn't have done a thing like that for nothing. Someone must have put him up to it. And what I was doing, Idris, was waiting to find who it was, and then bloody hammer them.'

'That's smart, Mustapha!' said Idris reluctantly. 'That's smart. But . . .'

'Yes, Idris?'

'Are you sure? About someone putting him up to it?'

122

'Look, Idris, it's not his territory, is it? He came from outside. So how did he know about it? A new hotel that wasn't even on his territory? The day after they moved in? Someone tipped him off, Idris, and I want to find out who it was.'

'Well, I'm with you there, Mustapha. But – couldn't it have been the police who tipped them off? Someone said it was the police.'

'But, Idris, again: it was our territory. The police know that as well as we do. Would they have let anyone else in on it? Would they?'

'Well, no . . .'

'And look at another thing: everyone in the quarter knows Chantale and her mother. You could say they were our people. Everyone knows that. Everyone here, that is. And they wouldn't like it. Our people! So they had to go outside the quarter to get someone to do it. Get someone like Ali Khadr, who wouldn't know any better. People here wouldn't like it. The police know that as well as anybody. I'm not saying that someone in the police might not have tipped them off, maybe told them that they'd moved in, that the moment was ripe. Although if they did, they'd do well to keep quiet about it. So you see, Idris, I'm not so stupid after all. There's someone behind this, and I want to find out who it is. *That's* why I was waiting!'

'Mustapha, you are a deep thinker!' said Idris in admiration.

'I am. And when I find out who set up the attack on the hotel, I'm going to cut their bloody balls off!'

'Just a minute,' said Seymour. 'What's this about a hotel?'

'The Miramar. The one Chantale and her mother run.'

'And what's this about an attack on it?'

'The day they moved in. The first day! Wrecked the place. Really did it over. It was shocking. My wife went round to give a hand in cleaning it up, and when she got back to me, she was going through the roof. "Call yourself a man?" she said. "And you let this sort of thing go on? In our quarter? Chantale and her mother. What sort of man are you?" I tell you, Idris, the beans weren't exactly good that night!'

'There was an attack on the Hotel Miramar? The night Chantale and her mother moved in?'

'That's right.'

'It sounds like a welcome party,' said Seymour.

'You know about welcome parties?'

'We have that sort of thing in England, too.'

'In England!'

Mustapha was impressed.

'They do it there, too?'

'Yes.'

Mustapha turned to Idris.

'There you are! It goes on all over the world. I've always said that. It's going global, I've always said.'

'Yes,' said Seymour, 'you'd be all right in England.'

(What was he saying?)

'But I think you'd better stay here,' he said hurriedly.

Ahead of him he saw a face he recognized.

'Dr Meunier!'

'Monsieur Seymour!'

Meunier stopped, and removed his hat, then mopped his brow.

'Hot today, isn't it? And getting hotter!'

'You've been on an errand of mercy?'

'You could call it that. I've been seeing old Ricard. You know Ricard? You may have seen him at the pig-sticking. Although you shouldn't have. One of these days he'll fall off and kill himself. Probably soon. Which would be a mercy for Suzanne.'

'His wife?'

'His daughter. Who looks after him lovingly. And with more patience than I could manage.'

He looked around.

'Fancy a drink?'

124

They went into a bar.

'A pastis, I think. With plenty of cold water. One for you, too?'

They sat down at a little table in the corner and sipped their drinks. Seymour had been going to go for beer but this was a less heavy alternative.

'So how are you getting on with your particular *chasse*?' asked Meunier.

'Less exciting than the pig-sticking,' said Seymour, 'and proceeding more slowly.'

'A lot of bother,' said Meunier, 'and to what purpose? People come and go, often quite quickly out here. Does it make a lot of difference in the end? Of course, as a doctor, I'm biased. I see too much of it.'

'Do you treat the military casualties, too?'

'Not in the field. They have their own doctors. But back here in Tangier. Usually for venereal diseases.'

'I should think that's likely to be a long job. Maybe like my job?'

'At least we both get paid for the work we do,' said Meunier.

They drank to that.

'Tell me,' said Seymour, putting down his glass, 'are you a pig-sticker yourself?'

'I was once,' said Meunier, 'but gave it up while the going was still manageable. Before I got too old. Unlike that old idiot, Ricard.'

'A veteran of the cause, is he?'

'You could say that. Rides every meet. And, actually, he's not too bad. Or, at least, he wasn't in his time. Now, of course, he's rather slower. But that's partly because Suzanne will only let him ride on a sensible old horse, which keeps him out of trouble. Fortunately it also keeps him out of the way of everyone else. "It's not you I'm bothered about, Ricard," I say. "It's everyone else." But, he says, they'd be all right if only he had a better horse! "Don't, for God's sake, let him get one," I say to Suzanne. Just been saying it, in fact.'

'You know,' said Seymour, 'I've been wondering about that. About the way the hunt goes. From what I could see, it spreads out a lot.'

'Oh, yes.'

'The better riders push on, the weaker drop behind.'

'Inevitably.'

'And, presumably, the same ones are always lagging behind?'

'I don't think they mind that too much. People like Leblanc and Digoin are just there for the ride. And there's nothing wrong with that. You get the benefit of the exercise, enjoy the air, the desert, sand, if you like that sort of thing.'

'So you find the same people taking up the rear each time? People like Digoin and Leblanc – oh, and, presumably Monsieur Ricard, too?'

'Yes. The same old stragglers. I won't mind confessing, though, that it's with a certain sense of relief that I see them come in each time. But they do!'

Seymour went to call on Macfarlane. He arrived just as Sheikh Musa was coming out of the Consul's office.

'I'm sorry, Musa,' Macfarlane was saying, 'but there's not much that I can do.'

'But there *is*; you're Chairman of the committee, aren't you?'

'Yes, but this doesn't come within the committee's brief.'

'Then why are you authorizing it?'

'We're *not* authorizing it. We're just sketching out the kind of arrangements that the Tangier zone will need to put in place for this to happen.'

Musa snorted.

'That's just legalistic quibbling!' he said. 'You know that once the committee has indicated the nature of the arrangements that will be likely, everyone will be shovelling things that way: money, guns, everything that is making Moulay stronger.'

'Look, I don't like it any more than you do. The man is just a bandit. But there's nothing I can do about it.'

'He's getting stronger all the time.'

'Yes, I know. But he's outside the projected zone and therefore nothing to do with me or the committee. He doesn't exist as far as we are concerned.'

'But that's ridiculous! If you go ahead with these "arrangements" –'

'Possibility of. We're just sketching out the possibilities, that's all.'

'– you'll have to make them *with* somebody. And that will be him.'

'We're not making arrangements with anybody. That comes later.'

'Building a railway line?'

'Making it possible to build a railway line. Once the zone has been declared. There will *need* to be a railway line, Musa, connecting Tangier with the south. All my committee is doing, Musa, is outlining the legal powers the Tangier council would need to be given for it to be able to conclude arrangements for such a railway to be built.'

'And make Moulay even stronger!'

'I agreed with you, Musa, it probably would. But that's not my concern. I have to look at things narrowly from the point of view of Tangier.'

'Who's looking at it from the point of view of Morocco?'

Macfarlane was silent. Then he shook his head.

'I'm sorry, Musa,' he said. 'These things go ahead.'

'The French, I suppose,' said Musa, answering his own question. 'The French!'

He saw Seymour and nodded to him. Then he turned back to Macfarlane.

'Do you know what I think?' he said. 'I think the French will do a deal with Moulay. I think they'll bring him back and make him Sultan in place of that other. Well, that might be no bad thing. The other has been useless. He has already given Morocco away. Moulay could hardly do worse. But you see what that would do? It would cement French control. And then there would be no more Morocco!'

He shook his head.

'And no one is doing anything about it!' he said.

He gave Macfarlane a quick embrace and stalked out. As he went, he nearly collided with Seymour.

'Ah, the Bossu man!' he said. 'Bossu! At least that was a step in the right direction!'

'Grand old boy!' said Macfarlane, looking after him. 'The trouble is, he can't accept that Morocco is changing.'

'He seems to me to have a pretty shrewd idea of what's going on.'

'Oh, he has that. But he can't accept – well, he can't accept that now it's inevitable. The French have taken over.'

'And there won't be a place for the likes of Sheikh Musa?'

'There would be a place for him. Lambert would be only too willing. But Musa's heart is with the older order, with the Parasol, you might say. And that has gone for good.'

He led Seymour into his office. There were the usual small teacups on the low table and a beautiful old teapot. Macfarlane lifted the lid and peered inside.

'Still some,' he said. 'Like some?'

The sharp smell of mint drifted into the room.

He poured some out for Seymour and filled his own cup.

'Now, what was it you wanted to see me about?'

'Three men,' said Seymour. 'Digoin, Leblanc and Ricard.'

'I know them, certainly,' said Macfarlane. 'But . . .'

He look puzzled.

'I'd like to talk to them.'

128

'Well, that can be arranged. But – laddie, are you sure you're not barking up the wrong tree?'

'No, I don't think so.'

'Because I know all three of them and the idea that they could have had anything to do with – which is, I take it, what you want to see them for . . . Look, Digoin is a danger on a horse, that is true. Especially with a lance in his hand. But that is because he is so short-sighted. He might stick anybody. Or anything. The idea that he might –'

'No, I wasn't thinking that.'

'And Leblanc is – well, he's one of the sweetest blokes around. He's a chemist, an apothecary, as they say here. Lovely chap. But wouldn't hurt a soul. Finds it hard to hurt even a pig. In fact, *never* hurts a pig. Never hurts anyone. Just rides along for the fun of it. And usually behind everyone so that there's no chance of being any-where near at a kill.'

'That's just why I want to see him.'

'Well, you know what you want, I suppose, but –'

'And Ricard?'

'Well, Ricard is one of the old settlers. And when I say old, I mean old. He must be in his eighties. He's still riding but even he recognizes he's got to watch it. Meunier's warned him. He's always warning him. "One fall, Ricard, and it will be the end of you!" But he loves it and won't give it up. He just rides along steadily behind the others. He's got a safe old nag, which is nearly as old as he is, and the two of them just keep going. He makes no attempt to keep up with the action these days –'

'Fine! That's just what I want.'

'Really?' said Macfarlane doubtfully.

'Yes, really.'

'Well, I'll take you over. It's not far. I'll take you over now if you like.'

Monsieur Ricard lived with his daughter in one of the villas just outside Tangier which Seymour had passed on his way to the pig-sticking. Her husband was in Customs and worked in the port of Tangier. Monsieur Ricard no longer worked and spent most of his days sitting on the verandah looking out over the bay. From time to time, however, he would rise from his seat and walk out into the garden, where he would find something to do or something to tell the gardener to do.

'Old habits died hard,' said his daughter, 'and he is still a farmer at heart. And he can't get used to not doing anything physical.'

'He still rides, though?'

His daughter pulled a face.

'Despite everything we can do.'

'What's that?' said Monsieur Ricard, whose hearing was not so much hard of as differential: some things he heard, some things he didn't. 'What's that about riding? The hunt's not been cancelled, has it?'

'No, Father,' said his daughter patiently. 'It's just that we are talking about it.'

'We? Who's we? You're not talking to that fool, Renaud, again, are you?'

'No, Father. It is Monsieur Macfarlane. And a friend. They want to talk about the hunt.'

'Well, bring them here, then. What are you waiting for? Hanging about, talking! *Bonjour*, Monsieur Macfarlane. Suzanne, bring in some coffee. You'll get some decent coffee here, Monsieur Macfarlane, that's one thing I will say for her.'

'Ricard, allow me to present a friend, Monsieur Seymour. From England.'

'What?'

'From England,' said Seymour, and then, shifting rapidly to ground where he thought Monsieur Ricard's hearing might be better: 'Allow me to say, Monsieur, that the view from your garden is remarkable!'

'Not bad, is it?'

'And the gardens! One could almost,' he said mischievously, 'be in England.'

'You'd do better here!'

Seymour laughed.

'I compliment you on your skill, Monsieur.'

'Well, well,' said Ricard, mollified. 'I don't do so badly, it is true. Do I, Macfarlane?'

'Not badly at all,' agreed Macfarlane.

'And you come to talk about the hunt?' Ricard said to Seymour.

'About a particular hunt,' said Macfarlane. 'Monsieur Seymour is a policeman and he is here to find out what happened to Bossu.'

'Bossu! Well, there's a fine fellow!'

'Monsieur Macfarlane suggested I talk to you, not only as someone who was there, but as someone familiar with the ways of the hunt.'

'Well, that's true,' said Ricard. 'I am. And that's more than could be said for Bossu. You know,' he said, turning to Macfarlane, 'I shall never understand how a man can ride week after week, year after year, and never learn a thing about hunting!'

'He wasn't interested,' said Macfarlane.

'No,' said Ricard, 'all he was interested in was showing off to Mademoiselle Monique.'

He chuckled maliciously.

'Not to Juliette, although she was there too. He didn't care a toss for Juliette, not once he'd married her.'

'Oh, I don't know –' said Macfarlane.

'It's true! the old man insisted. 'Not a toss. It was just a marriage of convenience. And they both got what they wanted. She wanted money, a house, and position. Her parents wanted money. And Bossu? Well, he got what he wanted, too: entry. Entry into the world of the Tangier social elite. For him, it wasn't the money, it was the social contacts. For them, it wasn't the contacts, it was the money. So they were all satisfied. Mind you, it nearly didn't happen. Did you know that?' he said to Macfarlane.

'No,' said Macfarlane, 'I didn't.'

'At the last moment they found out there was someone

else. Or had been someone else. Well, Juliette didn't mind that. It was all over now, and anyway the other woman had turned him down. But there was something else. The other woman was – well, quite unsuitable. So unsuitable as to reflect badly on Bossu. And, of course that meant on Juliette, and on her family, too. As I say, it was all in the past, but even so! Could the family condone this disgraceful, disgusting thing? It turned out, of course, in the end, that they could: for some more money.'

The old man cackled with glee.

'For more money!' he repeated. 'They could condone it then!'

He was convulsed with malicious pleasure.

'They could condone it then, all right! Mind you, it always rankled with Juliette. You see, the other woman, the one they all looked down on, had turned him down; and she, Juliette, hadn't!'

He slapped himself on the knee.

'You're talking about Monique?'

'No, no. Monique was after she'd turned him down. Before he knew Juliette. Lives up the hill, you know. Juliette. I'll bet she's not altogether sorry Bossu has gone.'

His daughter came in with a tray of coffee.

Evidently that needed explanation.

'Abdul was taking so long!' she said. 'So in the end I brought it myself.'

'Needs a good kick up the backside!' said Ricard testily.

'Thanks, Suzanne!' said Macfarlane. 'Children well?'

They talked about the children for a while. Monsieur Ricard concentrated on softening a biscuit in his coffee. Then he pushed his cup aside.

'So,' he said, looking at Seymour shrewdly, his eyes functioning, for this purpose at any rate, well, 'what do you want to know?'

Chapter Nine

No – contemptuously – he hadn't seen Bossu ride off at a tangent. He was already ahead of him at that point. In any case, he was riding on the other side of the course. Concentrating on the hunt. He liked to keep up with them while he could. Of course, in the end they would leave him behind, that was the penalty – with a baleful look at his daughter – of being lumbered with an old nag. If he had had Chestnut he would have kept up with them. Even been in at the kill!

'Chestnut is dead, Father,' said Suzanne quietly. 'He's been dead for years.'

'I know that!' he said impatiently. 'I'm just saying that with a proper horse I'd have kept up!'

'Of course, you would, Father, but –'

'She listens too much to that fool, Meunier!' Ricard growled.

'Sure, sure,' said Suzanne, and took the tray away.

'Well, there you are, Monsieur. I didn't see anything. I can't help you, I'm afraid.'

'Ah, but you can, Monsieur. It is afterwards that I am interested in. After Bossu had ridden away, and after he had been killed. Can I take you back to that earlier stage of the chase? And, perhaps, after. The riders would be bunched at the start, wouldn't they, all keeping up. But then they would begin to stretch out. Some of the slowest would be falling behind?'

'Well, of course! And I can tell you, they wouldn't have included me. Not if I had had a proper horse!'

'Not you, Monsieur, but, perhaps, the always slow riders, of whom you would have been aware –'

'Getting in the way. That fool, Digoin! And Leblanc. Why that man bothers to turn up at all, I cannot think. His head is in the clouds, Monsieur. He rides in a dream. He does not know, Monsieur, that it is a *hunt*. You chase the animal, yes? But not Leblanc. He is chasing rainbows! Or something the rest of us don't see.'

'Frustrating, frustrating!' said Seymour. 'But, Monsieur, I wondered if there was someone else. Someone, perhaps, who *was* a good rider, and a real huntsman, but who had, perhaps, joined the chase late? Who overtook the slower riders, even yourself –'

'He wouldn't have, not if I'd had a proper –'

'The others, perhaps, would not have been aware of it, but you, Monsieur, with your feel for the hunt and your sense of the chase as a whole, might well have noticed it. Someone coming up fast, and late . . .?'

Ricard thought.

'I think I was aware of someone doing that,' he said. 'Out of the corner of my eye. You understand, Monsieur, that at my age one cannot afford to take one's eye off – But, yes, I think I did notice someone coming up late.'

But, alas, Monsieur Ricard had few details to add. If he had seen someone, it had been only out of the corner of his eye. And that eye did not, perhaps, see as keenly these days as it once had done.

And Monsieur Digoin, that terror with the lance, although mostly to his own side, whom they called on afterwards, saw things, sadly, even more narrowly. In fact, he confessed shame-facedly, he didn't see much at all.

'It is wrong, I know,' he said, 'but I do like riding. I have ridden all my life, you see, and it is hard to give up now. I keep at the back. Out of the mêlée. I don't think I do any harm. The horse takes care of me. We are two old-stagers, fellow travellers, and we know each other. I rely on Agamemnon to bring me back. When he has had enough, then so have I.'

Had Monsieur Digoin been aware of a rider joining late? Alas, he wasn't aware of *any* other rider. He rode at the back, and his horse helped him from colliding with anyone else, but as for seeing them – well, Monsieur Digoin participated with enthusiasm but saw, as through a glass, darkly.

And Monsieur Leblanc, the over-mild Monsieur Leblanc? He was a sweetie and quite charming. But, alas, the French zeal for the chase, so extolled by Monsieur L'Espinasse, seemed to have gone quite missing in his case. He did, indeed, ride in a cloud, aware of little around him save the pleasant warmth of the sun, the whisper of the wind in his ears, the satisfying surge of the horse beneath him and, far off, the excited cries of the huntsmen.

'As in *The Seasons*,' he said.

The Seasons?

'Haydn's piece, you know. I've always thought the music very evocative.'

Well, yes. Yes. No doubt. But had Monsieur Leblanc seen –?

Someone joining late? Surely they had all started at the same time? He was always careful, himself, *not* to be late, it was such a nuisance to everyone else –

True, true, but possibly someone had unavoidably –?

Monsieur Leblanc, anxious to oblige, thought deep. And, yes, he thought he had been aware of someone coming up fast. Too fast. Going like the wind, that wind that whispered so soothingly in Monsieur Leblanc's ears, the wind that blew the overtaking rider's hair so straight behind him –

What?

Hair? Was Monsieur Leblanc saying that the rider was a woman?

Good heavens, no! It was just that as he had passed, Monsieur Leblanc had looked up, surprised, yes, surprised, he hadn't expected someone to be coming up so

135

fast behind him, and he had seen – well, he might not have seen correctly but this was what had struck him, the rider's long hair flowing back behind him –

On reflection, yes, it was puzzling. He couldn't think of anyone in the hunt with such long hair. He himself favoured short back and sides. And certainly the soldiers – well, they had their hair absolutely shaven! Maybe he'd got it wrong. It had all happened so quickly. The rider had come up from behind him, riding very fast. He hadn't seen him coming and then, suddenly, there he was! Passing him. He had overtaken him 'in a flash' and disappeared into the distance. But he had noticed –

Or had he noticed? It had all happened so quickly.

Had he noticed anything else apart from this one, astonishing, feature? Something about the clothes, perhaps? Or the horse? The colour of the horse, say?

It had all happened so quickly! The rider had passed 'as in a dream'.

As in a dream. Yes, knowing Monsieur Leblanc, Seymour could quite believe that!

The next morning when Seymour left the hotel there was no Mustapha and Idris outside waiting for him. In a way he was relieved, although he was also slightly disappointed. He had grown quite attached to them. But a bodyguard was hardly necessary. True, he had been glad of their aid when that pig had rushed out: but wild pigs were unlikely to be rushing out often, certainly not in the middle of Tangier, and he could see no other pressing need for defence. Their constant presence was, indeed, slightly embarrassing. How would it look to the people back at home if Macfarlane conveyed to them that two small-time crooks and drug dealers had lovingly attached themselves to their Man in Tangiers and devotedly followed him around wherever he went? So perhaps it was best –

But just at that moment Mustapha appeared round the corner.

'I am sorry, Monsieur, but you have to wait here. Idris has business.'

'Yes, well, I have business, too –'

'Idris's business,' said Mustapha, 'is your business.'

'My business?'

But Mustapha would say no more. They had to wait until Idris either arrived or sent a message. Mustapha sat down in the shade of the wall. Seymour stood around uncertainly for a while and then sat down on the hotel steps. He wondered if he should go inside and find somewhere more comfortable and less conspicuous to sit. Then he wondered why he was waiting, anyway. This, he couldn't help thinking, was another thing that wouldn't look good if word got back to the Foreign Office or Scotland Yard; their man hanging around at the behest of a couple of drug dealers!

Chantale came out of the door, saw him, raised an eyebrow, smiled (was it pityingly?) and then went back inside. To write, no doubt. But what was she writing? Her bloody gossip column, probably. Another, alarming, thought struck him. Might he not be about to figure in it? He would imagine all sorts of barbed comments about people out from London. And, meanwhile, ought he not to be getting on with –?

At that point a small boy appeared. He went up to Mustapha and whispered in his ear. Mustapha stood up.

'Right,' he said, 'we've got him!'

Exactly who had they got, wondered Seymour with misgiving? And what, in their world, did they mean by 'got'?

He would see, said Mustapha confidently, and they set off across the city with the small boy.

He led them to a large yard out of which carts were rumbling. A man was sitting glumly in the dust and Idris was standing over him ostentatiously fingering the dagger at his belt.

A man came out of the stables.

'Idris, I do this for you because you are my friend. But a cart has to be driven and –'

Idris held up a hand.

'It will be driven. Wait but a moment. My friends will be here and then – and here they are!'

'Don't worry, Mohammed!' said Mustapha soothingly to the man who had come out of the stables. 'This will not be forgotten.'

'I shall be out of a job,' said the man sitting on the ground. 'And that won't be forgotten, either.'

'Ten minutes, no more!' warned the man who had come out of the stables. 'No more!'

He went back inside.

'So, Fazal . . .' began Mustapha.

Fazal, it turned out, was the man Mustapha and Idris had spoken to at the pig-sticking, the man from whom they had got most of their information on that occasion. Dutifully, they secured his name and where he lived. And then, even more surprisingly, they had followed this up by calling on him to 'invite' him to come and meet their friend, who, they knew, was anxious to talk to him.

But when they had got to the block where he had said he lived they had been unable to find him. Yes, people in the block assured them, he certainly lived there but no one seemed to have seen him lately. Further inquiries led to a lady who claimed to be his wife. Yes, she said, he hadn't been around lately. He was a carter who worked irregular hours.

When might they catch him in?

Alas . . .

Does he not eat, inquired Mustapha, mindful, perhaps, that he was forgoing his own evening meal; and reckoning that after a day such as the carter worked, and after abstaining from food since daylight, one thing he would certainly not be missing was his evening Ramadan meal.

Well, of course . . .

Then they would see him then.

But when they had come again he was nowhere in sight. Nor was there much evidence of the preparation of a Ramadan meal.

You are mucking us about, said Mustapha severely.

No, no, no, no. That was the last thing she would do. It was just that . . . well, she had sensed, deep in her heart – she and Fazal were very close, she knew exactly what he would be thinking – and she had suddenly – belatedly, alas – realized that he would not be coming home that night.

Where would he be spending the night, then?

Alas, their closeness did not extend so far . . .

Mustapha, who did not believe a word of it, was all for cutting her throat. But Idris had had a flash of inspiration.

Could it be, he had asked sternly, that the pair were not actually married? And that Fazal had gone, as all right-thinking men should do, home to his real wife for the Ramadan evening meal?

The lady, flustered, agreed after a while that there could be something in what Idris had said.

So, Mustapha has asked, with rising impatience, where did Fazal and his true wife live?

Alas . . .

Mustapha had taken out his knife at this point, the lady had shrieked, the block had been aroused, people came swarming, and Mustapha and Idris had been obliged to beat a retreat.

Mustapha had been inclined to abandon their efforts: but Idris had suddenly had another flash of inspiration. He had remembered that the lady had let slip that Fazal was a carter. With a zeal for the chase which threatened to rival even that of the French, he had made a tour of all the carting establishments in the vicinity. Seymour, who realized what the effort must have cost him after the lateness of the day and his fasting, felt a moment's contrition after his earlier ruminations. Prize bloodhounds Mustapha and

139

Idris might not be but once they got on the trail they stuck to it. And in the end Idris had got his man.

'So, Fazal . . .' said Mustapha.

'I knew it meant trouble,' said the carter resignedly, 'when I heard that you were trying to find me.'

'Why did you make it difficult for us, then?' demanded Mustapha.

'Someone told me who you were,' said Fazal.

'Who we were?'

'That you were in the Business. No offence!' he added hurriedly. 'It was just that he thought it would be a good idea if I stayed away from you.'

'Well, that's not very friendly.'

'I would have been all right,' said the carter gloomily, 'if it had not been for Fatima.'

'Well, now we've found you,' said Mustapha, 'and it's not all right!'

'Ten minutes!' shouted the man who had gone back into the carter's. 'That's all! Then he's back on the carts!'

'Start talking!' ordered Mustapha.

The first part of Fazal's story Seymour already knew. He and a friend had been following the hunt and had seen Bossu ride off away from the others into the scrub. Fazal, who was evidently a keen student of form, and who had seen Bossu riding on previous occasions, had not wanted to follow him but his friend had persuaded him.

But then –

'Suddenly he wasn't there! "He's come off," I said to my friend. "I knew he was a dead loss. Let's get back to the others." "Perhaps he's broken his neck?" my friend said. "That would be worth seeing! Let's have a look." So we ran –'

'Just stop there for a moment,' said Seymour. 'You ran over. At once?'

'Yes. We guessed he'd come off and –'

'You got there pretty quickly?'

'Oh, we weren't slow.'

'And what did you see?'

'Him. With the lance sticking in him. And as soon as I saw that, I said, "Let's get out of here!" But my friend wanted to have a look. Close up. So –'

'Hold on. Back to the moment you first saw him. With the lance sticking in. What else did you see?'

'Well, there was nothing else. Just the bushes. And the sand. And the lance.'

'Yes, yes, I've got that bit. But there must have been other things.'

'I don't think so . . .'

'A horse, for instance?'

'Well, of course there was a horse. His.'

'What was it doing? Standing there?'

'No, no, it was running away. Bolting.'

'In which direction was it running?'

'Away. Straight ahead. Away from . . .'

'Away from the hunt? Think. Was it running back to the hunt or away from it?'

'Away from it.'

'You're sure about that?'

'Yes.'

'Because someone else I've talked to has said that they saw, or heard, a horse going back to the hunt.'

'If they did, that's not the horse I saw. The horse I saw was definitely bolting. Away from the hunt. The Frenchman had just come off –'

'Why? Why do you think he had come off?'

'Well, I don't know. Probably because he wasn't very good. The horse was all right, it was him. He would have had to swerve, you see, in and out of the bushes. They're very good, these horses, they know just what to do. They stick to the pig. Well, of course, if you're not much good as a rider, and with all that twisting and turning, it's no wonder if you come off –'

141

'You didn't see anything that might have *made* him come off?'

'Like what?'

'A snake.'

'We didn't see a snake.'

'Or someone in the bushes.'

'We didn't see anyone in the bushes. Of course, plenty of people came along afterwards –'

'No, no. At the moment he came off.'

'We didn't see anyone.'

'Because there must have been someone there. Or else how did the lance get stuck in?'

The carter was silent.

'I see what you mean.'

'There must have been a man there,' said Seymour. 'Very probably on a horse. You were there just afterwards. Are you sure you saw no one?'

The carter thought, but then shook his head.

'A horse is pretty big,' he said. 'We ought to have seen that. But we didn't.'

'Let me take you back again,' said Seymour. 'To the moment you suddenly realized that he'd come off. How far were you away from him at that point?'

'A couple of hundred yards. Three hundred, maybe.'

'Some way, then. And then you had to run, of course. So there would have been time for it all to happen. Time for a man who was following him in to get there and do it and then get away again.'

'He'd have had to have been quick,' said Idris.

'Yes, he certainly would. But now, Fazal, here's the question: there would have to have been another man following the Frenchman in. You were coming from that direction. Did you see him?'

The carter shook his head.

'No,' he said, 'I did not. Of course, I was running –'

'And the ground was uneven, I know. But it seems strange that another rider could have got there and away without you seeing anything of him.'

'Monsieur, it *is* strange,' said the carter earnestly, 'but –'

'It bloody *is* strange,' said Mustapha.

'Monsieur, I swear –'

'And I believe you,' said Seymour soothingly.

'If I could remember anything I would –'

'Take your time. Just try and see it all again in your mind.'

'Monsieur, I am trying, but . . .'

'Nothing?'

'Nothing.'

'I believe you. Go on searching your mind, and if anything comes, let me know.'

'Monsieur, I will. For you have spoken properly to me. Unlike some,' he added, with a look at Mustapha.

'Fazal –'

'And, Monsieur, I will ask my friend. For it may be that another pair of eyes will have seen something that mine missed.'

'Thank you, Fazal.'

The carter began to get to his feet.

'Fazal, there is just one other thing, a little thing, that perhaps you can help me on. When you got there, and you saw the Frenchman lying, there was a lance in his back –'

'That's right,' said Fazal, with relish.

'But was there not another lance somewhere? The Frenchman's own?'

'Are you going to be busy tonight?' asked Seymour, as they were walking back.

'Busy?'

'I was wondering if you were still expecting a visit from Ali Khadr.'

'No!' said Idris disgustedly. 'She's fixed it. Spoiled everything!'

'I tell you,' said Mustapha, 'when you get women *and* the mosque up against you, you can't do a thing.'

'You wouldn't have thought Ali Khadr would have listened,' grumbled Idris.

'Oh, he's very devout,' said Mustapha. 'Once she said she was going to the mosque, I knew there wasn't a chance.'

'Your mother must have a lot of influence,' Seymour said to Chantale.

'Oh, I don't know. She just knows a lot of people. But, then, she would, you see. She grew up in the quarter.'

'Yes, but –'

'I sometimes think there's a women's Mafia operating.'

'I thought women didn't have any power in Muslim countries.'

Chantale laughed herself silly. Then she recovered.

'Of course, she doesn't think of it as power,' she said. 'And nor do they. The men, I mean. They think they're the ones who make all the decisions. And I suppose in the end they do. But on the way there's a surprising amount of influence from the women.'

'You reckon?'

'Well, take this business of Ali Khadr, for instance. My mother goes round to the mosque and says: "You know about this raid, do you?" "Raid? What's this?" So they speak to Ali Khadr's wife, and she speaks to him. "What are you doing, you fool?" she says. "Don't you know you'll have the mosque up against you?" "I've got nothing against the mosque," said Ali Khadr. "And they've got nothing against me." "They will have," she says. "Hadn't you better think again?" So Ali Khadr thinks again. And – surprise, surprise! – comes to exactly the right decision.'

'Okay, I'll believe that. Especially after having seen the way Mustapha and Idris responded. But, look, in that case there's another question: if she was so well known in the quarter, how was it that the hotel was attacked?'

'You know about that?'

'Mustapha and Idris told me.'

'Yes, well, it did come as a nasty surprise,' she admitted. 'a shock, actually. We thought we were returning home, and then to find . . . I don't think they realized it was us. We had been away for quite a while, first in Algeria and then, well, all over the place after my father left the army. So we had lost touch with people, we'd forgotten how it was here.'

She laughed.

'When the hotel was raided, we even went to the police!'

She laughed again.

'Renaud! Can you imagine?'

'He didn't do anything?'

'Never does. We ought to have known better. We had come across him in Casablanca. It was a shock to find him here.'

'He was in Casablanca?'

'He was Chief of Police there.'

'At the time of the trouble?'

'Yes. I suppose,' said Chantale acidly, 'that they thought he did so well that they could safely promote him to being Chief at Tangier.'

'Have you seen the Chleuh dancers?' she asked.

'Dancers?'

She looked at her watch.

'They'll just have started. They're very good. Worth seeing. They're sort of like gypsies. They move around. Only they're not like gypsies in that they just do dancing. It's traditional dancing. They come from the Rif. I'll take you down.'

She called to her mother. There came an answering call from deep inside the hotel.

'I can't stay long,' Chantale said. 'I must give her a turn. They used to come to our farm. We would put them up, let them sleep in the barn. And that's where they would do their dancing. They like a firm floor. People would come from miles around. They would take it in turn to go round the farms. My father loved them. He had first seen them in the south. They used to visit the forts there.'

They were dancing this evening in one of the patios, of which there were surprisingly many. Almost all the large old Arab houses had one, but you might not know it because they were shut off from the street and the entrance was often quite small, marked only by a marvellously carved arch.

This patio was one of the larger ones. Already, though, it was crowded and people were spilling out on to the street. Because Seymour was tall, he could see over their heads. Chantale was quite tall also and good at worming and she worked a way through into the patio.

The dancers were all women. They were in long, beautifully decorated skirts and tight blouses. No burkas here! Their clothes clung to and revealed their supple figures.

Their faces, too. They had striking Arab, gypsy-like faces, with large eyes and straight dark combed-back hair, very Spanish-looking. But, of course, Spain was just across the straits and it could have been the other way round – the Spanish in that part of Spain were very Arab-looking.

They danced barefoot and the click of their feet on the tiles of the patio was as sharp as the crack of a whip. They danced with intricate, energetic foot movements. It was very like flamenco, Seymour thought; but then, why should it not be, with Spain so close?

They danced to the beat of a single drum, accompanied occasionally by a thin-wailing sort of flute, and, from time to time, the clashing of a tambourine.

The audience was an interesting mix. The poor people of the back streets were there, along with the better-to-do shopkeepers; but also businessmen from the big shops and offices of the better parts of Tangier, together with their wives.

Among the crowd were a number of soldiers, following intently.

'There're very popular with the army,' whispered Chantale.

'I'll bet!' said Seymour.

'No,' said Chantale reprovingly, 'it's not like that. The soldiers know the dances. And sometimes the dancers. They've come across them in the south.'

He saw de Grassac there, absorbed, like the others, clapping his hands in time with the clicks. And there, too, was Monique, and several of the other people he had seen in the Tent.

'I've got to go now,' whispered Chantale. 'I must let my mother have a turn.'

She slipped off through the crowd. Seymour remained, however, watching the dancers to the end.

It was only as they trooped off that he became aware of Mustapha and Idris standing faithfully near him.

'I'm sorry,' he said, 'I shouldn't have dragged you here.'

'Couldn't keep him away,' said Mustapha.

'It takes me back,' said Idris.

'You know the Chleuhs?'

'Grew up with them. In the mountains.'

He hesitated.

'I was just wondering . . .' he said.

'Yes, Idris?'

'If I might go and have a word with them.'

'I think there could be one or two people trying to do that, Idris.'

'To ask them about the village!' said Idris indignantly.

Chapter Ten

The next morning he went to find Mr Bahnini. The café across the road was empty.

'Not there yet, then?' he said to Mr Bahnini.

'Sadiq and his friends? They're still in bed. They think they're still at university.'

Seymour followed him into his office. He took out the scraps of paper he had found in Bossu's filing cabinet and laid them before him.

'Azrou, Immauzer and Tafilalet. Notice anything about these places?'

'They're all in the south.'

'And scattered. Not in a line, as I thought at first they might be. I thought they might be along the line of the projected railway and that Bossu might be going ahead fixing things. As he should have done in Casablanca. But, no, it couldn't be that. So what then?'

Mr Bahnini shook his head.

'Why might you go to them?'

'I'm afraid I don't –'

'People. They're about the only places in the interior with people, aren't they?'

'Tafilalet is really just an oasis,' said Mr Bahnini.

'But you'd need to go there, wouldn't you, if you were travelling around? And looking for people?'

'I'm afraid I don't see why Monsieur Bossu should be looking for –'

'Not Bossu. Someone else. Someone who is already down in the south. And wants people on his side.'

'You're suggesting –?'

'Moulay Hafiz. The Sultan's rebellious half-brother. Going from place to place, to all the big places, anyway, trying to build up support.'

'And Bossu?'

'Taking him something that he would need. Money. It would fit, wouldn't it? The dates show that Bossu visited the places at different times. Why? Because Moulay was there at different times – he was moving around. That would make sense, wouldn't it? He would want to talk to the local chieftains. He would need to stay in each place for a time, he would need time to persuade people. And he would need money. That's what Bossu was taking him.'

'Money from the north?'

'From people who sympathized with him. Or, perhaps, people who knew he would need to give something in return. Concessions, railway concessions, say, a building concession. People with a financial interest in the development of the south. And not just an interest in the south. If Moulay succeeded in gaining power, the whole of Morocco would be open to things. This was big. Big rewards, and, probably, big interests, in search of them. Whom, possibly, Bossu had been working for since Casablanca.'

Mr Bahnini considered.

'It is possible,' he conceded. 'Moulay Hafiz is certainly trying to build up support.'

'For which he would need money.'

'For which, yes, he would need money.'

'Which Bossu might have been taking him.'

'He might indeed.' Mr Bahnini hesitated. 'But, sir . . .'

'Yes?'

'How are you going to confirm it? And – forgive me, sir – there is another thing. Even if you did confirm it – perhaps you will think it not my place to make this observation? – but, even if you did confirm it, what bearing would that have on Mr Bossu's death? Which, I take it, sir, is what you are really interested in?'

149

'It might explain why someone wanted to kill him: to stop him.'

By the time he left the committee's offices, Sadiq and his friends had taken up their usual position in the café. They waved to him to join them.

'Just for a moment, perhaps . . .'

But he rather enjoyed being with them. He liked the splendid conversation about ideas of the young and envied them their opportunities at university. Nothing like that for him. And in the East End, if you were at all bright, you were rather conscious of that. It was a poor area and no one from there went to Oxford or Cambridge. Yet many of the immigrants from the Continent had had some sort of education, even been to university, and they brought with them an immense interest in ideas. There was plenty of intellectual discussion in the East End, in the Working Men's Clubs and the anarchist discussion groups.

Not so much in his own family. His grandfather had been agin the government in Russia and Poland but that had been an emotional matter rather than an intellectual one. Seymour's mother, who had learned the hard way in Austro-Hungarian prisons what the discussion of ideas could lead to, shrank now from engaging with them too closely. His father, who had learnt the same lesson, now kept resolutely away from politics of any kind and concentrated on business. Only in Seymour's sister did the revolutionary passion of their grandparents burn on. She was a member of every dotty organization the East End could provide, and there were many of them: feminist, socialist, trade union, teachers' – she was a teacher herself, and had dragged Seymour as a young boy, not altogether unwillingly, from one meeting to another. And then been crushingly disappointed when he had joined the police.

Not much intellectual discussion in the Mile End police station! But Seymour's linguistic gifts had led to him being put in the Special Branch and used principally with the

East End's many dissident groups. Frightening to some, and especially the government: but when you got to know them, frightening to no one else.

So Seymour was used to groups like the present one and not alarmed, amused by them, rather, and tender towards them as to the young.

The conversation was on lines similar to the one they had been having the last time he had met them. They questioned him eagerly about the revolution in Istanbul and were interested, and a little depressed, when he told them that his impression was that the people most instrumental in making it were the young officers in the army.

'No chance of that happening here,' they said dejectedly. 'The army's French.'

At one point he realized that they were all speaking in French. He thought at first that this might be out of consideration for him but then understood that this was how they habitually spoke. It seemed odd, a bunch of young Moroccan nationalists and yet all speaking French. Then he saw that this was part of their problem.

'It will have to come from someone else,' someone said.

Awad banged his hand on the table.

'We shouldn't be talking like this!' he said. '"It will have to come." That's no way to talk. It's too passive. We should be saying, "This is the way we're going to do it!" We shouldn't be leaving it to others. *We* should be doing something.'

There were mutters of agreement. Then –

'Well, we are, aren't we?' said someone.

There was a sudden awkward silence.

Seymour began to get up.

'Perhaps I'd better leave you to carry on your discussion.'

'No, no, please . . .'

But the discussion was ending anyway.

Sadiq got up from the table, too.

151

'I've got to go and see Benchennouf,' he said. 'I promised I'd call in this morning. There are some proofs he
wants me to correct.'

He went round the group shaking hands, in the French
way: and then, when he came to Seymour, he hesitated, a
little shyly.

'Would you like to come with me?' he blurted out.

'Who is Benchennouf?'

'He's an editor.'

'He's Sadiq's editor!'

'You work for a newspaper?' said Seymour curiously.

'Well, not exactly work – I don't get paid, or anything.
But I do things for them.'

'And sometimes he gets a piece in!' said someone
proudly.

'Well . . .'

'Do come!' said Sadiq. 'You'd like Benchennouf. He's
very knowledgeable.'

'And very interesting.'

'Yes, do go!' they urged.

'He was in Casablanca,' someone said.

'Yes, I'd like to,' said Seymour.

Sadiq led him through ever narrower and increasingly
dingy streets.

Mustapha and Idris closed in.

'Hey, where are you taking him?'

'It's all right,' said Seymour. 'They're friends of mine.'

Sadiq looked at them doubtfully.

'We're going to a newspaper office,' he said, however,
sturdily.

'What, here?' said Mustapha disbelievingly.

'That's right. In Al-Abbassiya Street.'

'Look, I know Al-Abbassiya Street and there aren't any
newspaper offices there.'

'Yes, there are. *New Dawn*, it's called.'

'I know Ali's, and Mother Mina's and then there's the baker at the end – but *newspaper*?'

'It's not one of those . . . is it?' said Idris. 'Hey, you're not taking him to one of those indecent places?'

'Certainly not!' said Sadiq indignantly.

'It's not Mother Mina's, is it?' said Mustapha.

'I wouldn't have thought she was into that sort of thing,' said Idris. 'Plain and simple is more her line.'

'It's not a place like that!' cried Sadiq furiously. 'It's a *newspaper* office. An important newspaper. *New Dawn* is what it's called.'

'*New* . . .?'

Seymour, when they got there, could understand how Mustapha and Idris might have missed it. It was a single small room in a dilapidated building with one desk and a typewriter. Dawn, it appeared, had still some way to go.

Mustapha and Idris exchanged glances.

'We'll be just outside,' they told Seymour, and took up position on either side of the door.

A man was sitting at the desk, smoking.

'I've brought a friend, Benchennouf,' said Sadiq. 'Monsieur Seymour, from England.'

'I am pleased to meet you, Mr Seymour,' said Benchennouf, in English, extending a hand. He seemed relieved, however, when Seymour replied in French.

Everything in the place was familiar to Seymour, the small, dingy office, the single typewriter on the desk, the political pamphlets around the walls. The East End was full of such places. Many of the people there had a background in radical politics on the Continent and not a few of them had been journalists. When they had arrived in London they had seen no reason why they should not continue their activities and had set up small presses from which they could continue the good fight.

Seymour was always being sent to such places and took a relaxed view of them. His own sister worked in about four of them. *New Dawn* was no different. It was, he soon worked out, a radical nationalist journal: anti-French but

153

also anti-Sultan. It advocated things that in other countries would be taken for granted: an elected Parliament, for instance, and freedom from arbitrary imprisonment.

Benchennouf, too, he thought he had worked out. He was an educated man (educated at a French university, Sadiq told him later, with some pride) and had the interest in ideas typical of the French intellectual. Seymour could see his appeal to young, university-educated men like Sadiq.

'So how do you come to be in Morocco, Mr Seymour?' Benchennouf asked.

Seymour told him.

'Police!' said Benchennouf, looking accusingly at Sadiq.

'The *English* police,' said Seymour quickly. 'And don't ask me,' he said, laughing, 'why an Englishman should be investigating a Frenchman's death. In a country which is neither France nor England!'

He shrugged.

'I suppose,' he said, 'it is because Bossu's death is, in a way, an international matter, since he was Secretary of that committee. And maybe they didn't want it investigated by a Frenchman.'

'Nor the Mahzen,' said Benchennouf. 'Well, I can understand that.'

'You know about the committee, of course?'

'Of course. In fact, when it was set up, I wrote to it. I said that the committee was improper and illegal and that Morocco could not accept any decision that it might make. I got no reply. Naturally.'

'Have you ever met Bossu?'

'I didn't meet him over this but I'd come across him earlier. But I didn't trust him. Not after Casablanca.'

He turned to Sadiq.

'I went for him then, you know, really went for him. Of course, a lot of people did, but I flatter myself that it was *New Dawn* that really made an impact. We were able to publish details, you see. Details of the contracts. Of course, by themselves they didn't tell much but I was able to point

154

out the understandings that lay behind them. I demanded that they be made explicit. Of course, they wouldn't do that. They said that it was all in the contracts. It wasn't, of course. As we pointed out. And then we told everybody what wasn't in the contracts.

'They didn't like that, I can tell you. Not one little bit. We had the police round, and then some other men who weren't exactly the police. We were never quite sure who they were. We asked, but they wouldn't tell us. But they spoke French.

'So in our next number we asked who were these foreigners who broke into Moroccan property and knocked people about. But then they came back and really smashed the place up and I had to get out in a hurry. I went to Rabat for a year. And by the time I got back it was all over.'

He looked at Seymour.

'That was how I first came across Bossu. Actually, I didn't know at the time how much he was involved. It only came out later. If I had known then, what a story it would have made! But it didn't come out until later, years later, and then only in dribs and drabs. It never quite all came together and I could never quite make use of it.

'But then when they announced his appointment as Secretary of that outrageous committee, then I could see how to do it. So I wrote that piece. Did you see it? No, of course you wouldn't have done, you weren't even in the country. I put it in *New Dawn* and splashed it around all over the place and I think it had quite an impact.

'I wouldn't be surprised if – well, you should never make such claims, I know, but – if it might not have had some bearing on what happened to him. It brought it all back to people's minds. And maybe it put it into someone's head to . . .'

He gave a little, self-satisfied smile.

'You are looking for the person who killed Bossu, Monsieur Seymour. Well,' he leaned forward and placed his hand theatrically on his breast, 'I think I can claim some of the credit at least for that particular service.'

When he came out of the office with Sadiq, Mustapha and Idris closed in again.

Sadiq was alarmed.

'What are you doing?'

'Looking after him,' said Mustapha. 'Which is more than you're doing bringing him to a place like this.'

'It's a newspaper office!' protested Sadiq indignantly.

'Oh, yes!'

They walked on a little way in silence. Then –

'What's your newspaper like, then?' asked Idris.

'It's sort of . . . political.'

'Political!'

'Then he *has* been taking you to the wrong sort of place!' said Idris. 'You want to keep away from anything like that.'

'Have you no shame?' cried Sadiq, touched nearly and aroused despite himself. 'Keep away from politics? At a time like this!'

'What's this about the time?'

'When the French have imposed a Protectorate on us?'

'What's that?'

'Protectorate. You know about the Protectorate. Don't you?'

'I think I've heard something,' said Mustapha vaguely.

'They're taking over Morocco!'

'The French?'

'Yes.'

'I thought they *had* taken over Morocco?'

'Look, it'll make no difference to us,' said Idris.

'Oh, yes, it will. There'll be soldiers everywhere.'

'There are now,' said Mustapha.

'There'll be more!' promised Sadiq. 'And police.'

'Police?'

'Real police. French police!'

'That could be a problem,' admitted Mustapha.

'Naow,' said Idris. 'Just offer them more.'

'You don't understand!' cried Sadiq. 'It will be different. The French will be running everything. Everything!'

'Good luck to them.'

'They'll be in control!'

'Not a chance!' said Idris dismissively.

'We'll be all right,' said Mustapha.

'Is that all you think of?' said Sadiq hotly. 'Have you no pride? Have you no thought for Morocco?'

'Morocco?'

'You're a Moroccan, aren't you?'

'Not me,' said Mustapha. 'I'm from the Rif.'

'But that *is* –'

'And I'm a Berber,' said Idris.

'We're *all* Moroccans!' cried Sadiq desperately. 'And we must stand together and fight the French.'

'Fight the . . .?'

'French, yes.'

'Soldiers?'

'If necessary.'

'He's mad!' said Mustapha.

There was a silence. Then –

'Is that what this newspaper of yours is all about?'

'Well, yes.'

'Stand up against the French? And get your heads blown off? Thank you very much!'

'If we don't fight now, we'll never –'

'Listen, laddie: do you know what fighting *is*?'

'Well –'

'Me,' said Idris virtuously, 'I don't want to fight anybody. I just want to get on with my work.'

'Well, of course, everyone – But . . . What is your work?'

'Well, we do a bit in kif –'

'Kif!'

'Yes. Run the occasional load. Spread it around. That sort of thing.'

Sadiq was silenced for a moment. Then, as they walked on, he whispered to Seymour:

'These are not good people, Mr Seymour. I feel I should tell you.'

They were going through a particularly squalid part of the city, a warren of narrow little twisting streets, and for the first time Seymour was glad that he had Mustapha and Idris with him. They closed in on him so that they stood touching shoulder to shoulder. Sadiq was plainly uneasy and pressed in on them too.

It soon became apparent, however, that his uneasiness was prompted by a different cause than theirs. The houses in this part of the city were old and decaying. Their walls were crumbling and scarred as if attacked by leprosy and they had no windows. They had doors, however, and in the doorways people were standing. More precisely, and this was the source of Sadiq's discomfort, women were standing.

These, too, were not 'good people'. They moved forward as the three men passed and muttered something presumably inviting but from which Sadiq shrank back. He kept his eyes fixed straight before him as if a look or a touch or even a listen was polluting.

From behind the women in the open doorways came the fumes of cooking fat. Even here, thought Seymour, they were preparing the end-of-fast Ramadan meal. The smell of the burning fat blended with the strong smell of excrement which assailed him whenever they went past one of the putrid alleyways, strewn with refuse and rotting vegetables, which went off the street at irregular intervals.

Yet you could get it wrong. Sometimes when you looked up the alleyway you caught a glimpse of a beautiful old façade, a piece of exquisite wood carving, or even a tiny, perfect Moorish patio with delicate balconies and colonnades.

Some of the doorways had quaint inscriptions painted

above them. Several of them, for instance, had printed the words: '*Maison honnête*', a decent house. Strange, that people should so feel the need to proclaim their virtue. And in French, too!

They were going through a warren of particularly filthy, dark, narrow, twisting streets when suddenly, high above them, something flashed. He looked up and saw to his surprise the glinting, coloured tiles of the minaret of a mosque catching the sun and realized that they were just behind the Kasbah.

Sadiq saw his surprise and misinterpreted it.

'It is wrong,' he said indignantly, 'that such people should be allowed to be so near the Kasbah! We have complained about it but nothing has been done. We went to the Préfet again only last week demanding that those dreadful women be removed. Perhaps they should be put in a reserved quarter near the barracks, not near a holy place. But every day another house is turned over to one of those places where they work. It is disgraceful! Think how it must be for the children, and how humiliating it is for decent people to have such neighbours.'

And now Seymour understood the significance of the inscriptions he had seen above the doors: '*Maison honnête*', a valiant attempt by the 'decent people' to distinguish themselves from their indecent neighbours!

The puritanical Sadiq compressed his lips and walked on, keeping his eyes fixed straight ahead.

He brought Seymour dutifully back to the spot from which they had set out and then hung around for a moment.

'I hope you found Benchennouf interesting,' he said awkwardly.

'Oh, I did. Thank you for taking me.'

'He's not – not to everyone's liking. But he's different, don't you think? He stands out against opinion. We need people like him in Morocco today.'

'Indeed, yes. Perhaps, yes.'

'I count myself fortunate to be among his friends. And he's given me my chance, you know. A start. As a journalist.'

'I wish you every success.'

'Some say that *New Dawn* is nothing much –' he looked daggers at Mustapha and Idris – 'but I think it is a good place to be. It is not like the other newspapers. They're all prisoners, prisoners of the French. *New Dawn* stands out against them. Against the French, and against the Sultan. And for Morocco. My father thinks that *New Dawn* is just a joke. But he doesn't understand. We need papers like that if Morocco is to survive. And journalists like Benchennouf. I hope to be one,' he confided.

'A small newspaper is a good place to learn the ropes,' said Seymour.

'Yes, it is. I think so. That's just what I said to my father. And what is so good, what is so useful, is that Benchennouf brings wider perspectives. He worked on a paper in France, you know. After he had finished at university. He went to a university in France, you know. A lot of people who do that don't come back here. But he did, and all credit to him. I've thought about going to a university in France. To do something post-graduate. But if I did, I would come back here afterwards. Morocco must not be abandoned.'

'No, indeed.'

Sadiq seemed pleased by Seymour's encouragement.

'That's what Benchennouf always says. "Morocco must not be abandoned." Awad sometimes talks about going abroad but Benchennouf says he shouldn't. "Your place is here," he says. And he's got a right to say that because he came back himself.

'"If you're here," he says, "you can respond at once when you're needed." As he was in Casablanca. That was an awful time. The French were all screaming at us. Only Benchennouf stood up against them. I used to read every number of his paper as soon as it came out. I was at school at the time. And when they arrested the man who was selling *New Dawn* just outside the school, I took over. I was so angry, so angry at what they were doing, that I wanted to do something. And did until Benchennouf was chased out.'

'Tell me about Casablanca at the time.'

'It was horrible. They weren't just beating people, they were shooting them! I saw two people once and they were dead! They had called the army in and they were *shooting*. And no one said anything! Apart from Benchennouf.'

'And Chantale's father, I gather.'

'Captain de Lissac. Oh, he was wonderful. I so admired him! In fact, for a time I hero-worshipped him. We all did, at school. We thought he was so brave. To stand up like that! Even though he was a Frenchman and a soldier. But then they hounded him out, too.'

'Well, I can understand that,' said Seymour. 'He was, after all, a soldier and soldiers have to do what they're told. Or else you don't have an army.'

'Yes, but you can't just do what you're told. Sometimes you have to go by, well, bigger things. Well, I think that, anyway,' he said, suddenly overcome by embarrassment.

'I think it does you credit,' said Seymour.

'Thank you. Well, thank you . . .'

Sadiq lapsed into tongue-tied silence.

But then he burst out again.

'But what I can't see is why they had to be so nasty to him. You ought to be able to disagree without being nasty. But they couldn't. And it went on and on. They couldn't leave him alone. Even after he had stopped speaking out. "Come on," some people said. "That's enough!" And the army began to say that, too. At least, that's what people said. People began to say that there must be something more in it, something personal. Something personal between de Lissac and Bossu.'

'Why did Bossu come into it?'

'Well, he had been organizing things on the company side. I don't really understand that bit, you'd have to ask

161

Benchennouf. But I suppose that brought them up against each other and maybe that was enough. But it seemed to go further than that. There was a sort of campaign against Captain de Lissac, and people said that Bossu was organizing it. We tried to organize a counter-campaign, but, of course, we were just schoolboys . . .

'The headmaster spoke to our parents, and my father said it had to stop. I didn't want to but my mother said it would only make things worse for Captain de Lissac.

'It was a terrible time in our household, too. My mother was strongly in favour of Captain de Lissac. All Moroccans were. But, of course, my father worked for Bossu! Our friends, neighbours, stopped speaking to us. I realize now that it was very hard for my father. I suppose that, deep down, he admired Captain de Lissac as much as anybody. But he couldn't say anything, he had to remain loyal to Bossu. Or, at least, quiet. And I don't suppose I made things any easier for him.

'But it wasn't just Moroccans who objected to this campaign against him. A lot of the French did, too. This is going too far, they said. That's when people began to mutter that there must be something personal in it. "There's more in this than meets the eye," they said. Because Bossu seemed almost demented. People said that it was because Bossu liked to have his own way and the Captain had tried to put a spoke in his wheel. But others said no, that there was bad blood between the two, that there was a history of this.

'Well, I don't know about that. All I know is that I thought the Captain was a hero. And Benchennouf, too. He was willing to stand up for Morocco. Unlike some,' said Sadiq with a baleful glance at Mustapha and Idris.

Chapter Eleven

'Well!' said Monique. 'This *is* a surprise! A pleasant surprise, I must add. But, nevertheless, a surprise. I took it for
granted that you, like everyone else, were putting me up
on the shelf. Where, to be fair, I probably belong.'

'I couldn't resist taking you down again.'

'Thanks! I was just getting used to independence. But
independence is a strange thing, isn't it? All my life I've
pursued independence, it was the first thing I wanted, to
get away from my parents. Then I wanted to be a woman
on her own, a real free spirit. Then I wanted to get away
from a man because, tied up with him, there was no
independence. Every decision I've made I've tried to go for
independence. And where do I finish up? Less free than
half the boring married women of Tangier!'

Seymour laughed.

'It's coming,' he said. 'It's coming. I can feel it.'

'Oh, good. Would you like a drink? Come out on to the
balcony. Then we can talk. That is what you've come for,
I presume. It's not for my worn face and jaded eyes.'

'You're quite right. It is what I have come for. And I'd
like a whisky, please. And, actually, it is your worn face
and jaded eyes that have brought me here. Because they
speak of experience, a woman's experience, and that's just
what I need.'

'Good gracious! Your plight must be desperate indeed.
I'll bring the whisky quickly.'

She brought the whisky, two glasses, and sat down
beside him. The sun had moved round her little balcony

so that they were unable to sit in the shade but it was already losing its heat. Out in the bay the glitter had gone off the sea.

'Now tell me,' she said, 'because I'm all agog to know what, in this country of men, leads you to think that a woman could have anything valuable to contribute.'

'Almost everyone I've talked to,' said Seymour, 'has taken it for granted that Bossu's death was tied up with politics. That it had nothing to do with his personal history. Now why is that?'

'Morocco is a very political country. Especially just at the moment.'

'Sure. I can see that. And the temptation is to say, since he was so much bound up with these politics, that he died because of it. But might it not be something more personal?'

'Like what?'

'Love.'

'Jesus! The things you say! Love? What's that? Tell me about it.'

'Bossu had a complicated love life.'

'Not very. I was in a separate compartment. In all senses. And his wife was a simple soul.'

'Maybe. But I've heard the officers. They were all after her. And I'll bet there were others.'

'She liked it like that.'

'I'm sure.'

'She had a thing about officers. It used to drive Bossu mad.'

'In general? Or was there one in particular?'

'Not that I know of. The point is, though, that they were admirers not lovers – Juliette is a great tease.'

'Perhaps there *was* a note of disillusion in what they said.'

'She liked to lead them on and have them panting. And then withdraw.'

'How unsatisfactory! You don't think, then, that in

164

the tangled tease life there was an affair so serious as to . . .?'

'I don't think there was anything serious in Juliette's life, love or otherwise. Perhaps money. Oh, and certainly vanity. But perhaps you shouldn't ask me. Is a spurned mistress an objective source of information?'

'Were you spurned?'

'Not really. Except that he didn't marry me.'

'She sees you as a rival.'

'And I, her.'

'That, actually, is why I've come to you. You are likely to know anything to her discredit. And more than likely to be willing to tell me about it.'

Monique laughed.

'I hadn't thought of that,' she admitted. 'But, even with all these advantages as a source of information, I am going to disappoint you. I know of no private affair which might have had a bearing on Bossu's death. If that is what you are asking.'

'No one, you see, has ever mentioned that as a possibility.'

'That, in a place like Tangier, is telling. But if you have doubts, why don't you ask Renaud? This, at least, is one part of the investigation which he will have researched thoroughly.'

She went away for a moment to refill their glasses and Seymour sat thinking.

'All right, then,' he said, when she came back. 'Let me try another thing on you. It is about Bossu himself. You told me, when I talked to you before, about Casablanca, and I realize now how important that was in the recent history of Morocco. And how important it was to Bossu. But there was another person to whom it was important too: Chantale's father, Captain de Lissac. And between the two there was considerable animosity.'

'No,' said Monique.

'No?'

165

'On Bossu's part, yes, perhaps. But on de Lissac's part, no. I think initially he might not even have been aware of Bossu's existence.'

'You surprise me.'

'Bossu always stayed in the background. He was active, yes, but behind the scenes. I think it quite likely that it was only afterwards that the Captain realized who he had been up against. Remember, he had never been to Casablanca before. He knew nothing about Casablanca people or politics, and probably didn't want to. He was a soldier, and he saw things in clear-cut terms, right or wrong. To him it was a moral issue and not a political one. It was never as complicated as politics.'

'And so he went straight ahead?'

'That's right.'

'And crossed Bossu. And didn't even know he had done it. Is that what you are telling me?'

'Yes. I think so.'

'Why, then, the animosity? Because from what I have been told there was animosity, and a lot of it.'

'Yes, there was animosity. Bossu hated him. I don't know why. It surprised me at the time. Why all this venom, I asked him? Because I quite liked de Lissac. He seemed a decent man. But Bossu nearly bit my head off. He shouted at me – something he did very rarely – and told me I didn't understand these things, that I didn't know anything about it. So after that I shut up. But I was surprised, yes, at the intensity of his feelings. I thought it was perhaps because he had slipped up and was angry with himself. But, yes, it was more than that.'

'I wondered, you see, if there was some past history.'

'Not that I know of. But there could have been. Look, why don't you ask old Ricard. You know Ricard? He's a –'

'Yes, I know him.'

'Well, he's an old gossip but he's been around a long

time and there's little about Tangier that he doesn't know. Why don't you have a word with him?'

But first there was something else he had to do. He tried the barracks but they told him that de Grassac, along with most of the officers, was out training. Seymour was impressed by this but then learned that what the training was was for the pig-sticking that Saturday. So he went over to the Tent.

The soldiers had just got back from their training and were seeing to their horses. Most of them were watching a long line of horses that were going past the Tent, escorted by some of Musa's white-gowned riders and by Musa himself.

'Beautiful, aren't they?' said Millet, who was standing beside Seymour. 'I will say this for Musa, he breeds some of the best.'

'They're mounts for the army, are they?'

'I wish they were. But I don't think so.'

Instead of entering the roped-off enclosure at the back of the Tent, the horses went on past and stopped at a point some distance away.

'They're for someone else,' said Millet. He laughed. 'Who is probably paying more.'

Several of the officers had left their horses to study them. One of the officers strode across to Musa.

'Who are those for, Sheikh Musa? I don't suppose we could persuade you to think of the army?'

'I'm delivering some to you tomorrow.'

'They won't be as good as these, though, will they?'

Musa looked the horses over.

'These *are* good,' he said with pride.

'A special price, too, I'll bet!' said someone.

'Sheikh Musa, I'd pay a special price. I'd be prepared

167

to go over the odds for one of these. Privately, never mind the army.'

Sheikh Musa patted him on the arm.

'I'll look one out for you. Next week, when I'm over. But these are all bespoke.'

He patted the officer again.

'You've got an eye for a horse, Vibert, I know that,' he said. 'I'll look one out for you.'

'Where are they going?' asked Seymour.

'Down south, probably,' said Millet. 'Moulay would give his right arm for some of these.'

Sheikh Musa overheard and turned on him fiercely.

'They're *not* going to Moulay!' he said furiously.

'Sorry, sorry, sorry, Sheikh Musa!' said Millet hastily.

'You only give a good horse to a good man!' said Musa severely.

'Right!' said Millet. 'I'm with you all the way on that. You know that.'

'Well, I suppose I do,' said Musa. 'I just don't like it to be thought –'

'We don't!' said Millet quickly. 'We really don't. When I said south, I wasn't thinking of Moulay.' He turned to Seymour, anxious to deflect Musa's wrath. 'You've heard about Moulay, have you?'

'The Sultan's half-brother?'

'By a slave girl!' grunted Musa. 'Not by a wife. And it shows.'

'Causing trouble, I hear.'

'It's not the trouble he's causing now,' said Millet. 'The army can contain that. It's the trouble he might cause in the future. Isn't that right, Sheikh Musa?'

'If the French have their way.'

'Oh, come, Sheikh Musa! I don't think they like him any more than we do.'

'Then why are they cosying up to him?'

'But are they?'

'Yes,' said Musa shortly. 'They are.'

168

'Ah, well,' said Millet, backing off hastily. 'I wouldn't know about that.'

'The mistake they're making,' said Musa, 'is changing the man they're backing. They ought to stick with the one they've got. He's no good, I agree, but you can't be changing all the time. There's got to be some consistency somewhere.'

'You don't supply mounts to caravans going down south, Sheikh Musa, do you?' asked Seymour.

'I used to. But not since Moulay got down there. Why do you ask?'

Seymour decided to risk it.

'I'm still on Bossu,' he said. 'And I think Bossu made several trips to the south. Taking money. For which he would need mounts.'

'Camels,' said Sheikh Musa. 'Not horses.'

'He would have needed a bodyguard, too.'

He found Sheikh Musa studying him.

'Taking money,' said Sheikh Musa, 'to Moulay. Is that right?'

'I suspect so.'

'Well, not on my horses.' He was quiet for a moment or two. Then he said: 'You've found that out, have you?'

'I think so. I'm trying to confirm it.'

'You don't need to confirm it,' said Sheikh Musa. 'I'm telling you.'

'If you say so, Sheikh Musa,' said Seymour, 'that has weight for me.'

Musa continued to study him, then grunted.

'I would have tried to see he didn't get horses,' he said. 'Or camels, for that matter. But there are too many people in the game. Everyone's running things down south. He would have got them somehow or other. The only way to stop someone like Bossu is the way someone did stop him.'

He laughed.

'You're still looking for the person who did it, are

169

you? Well, don't look too hard. Whoever did it, did a good job.'

Among Musa's white-gowned men was the tall Arab, Ahmet, whom he had seen convoying horses through the middle of Tangier with Millet. He went across to him.

'Are you going to be busy again on Saturday, Ahmet?'

There was a flash of white teeth.

'As always when there is a pig-sticking.'

'First, the pigs, and then the hunt. Is that right?'

'That's right,' Ahmet agreed.

'When you ride beside the hunt, keeping an eye open for those who fall, is there somebody doing the same on the other side of the hunt?'

'Oh, yes. For sometimes a horse or a pig can run off in that direction.'

'When the Frenchman came off, you were riding on the north side of the hunt, is that not so?'

'That is so.'

'Do you remember who were the outriders on the south side on that occasion?'

'I do. Ibrahim and Riyad.'

'Are they here?'

Ahmet looked around.

'No,' he said.

'Will they be here at the pig-sticking on Saturday?'

'Oh, yes. They are good men. I like to use them.'

'I will speak to them then.'

De Grassac came out of the Tent.

'Good practice?'

'Yes, thank you.' De Grassac looked around. 'Just the day for it,' he said. 'Fresh. Not much wind.'

'That makes a difference, does it?'

'Blows the sand up into your eyes. That doesn't matter much. But sometimes it affects the horses.'

'Do you think I could have a look at your lance?'
De Grassac looked surprised but passed it to him.
'Can you tell one lance from another?'
'They're all pretty much the same. Some are heavier.'
'I remember you said that you'd got the lance that was used to kill Bossu?'
'Yes,' said de Grassac. 'That's right.'
'Have you still got it?'
'Yes. Of course. I'm keeping it in case anyone wants to look at it. Renaud, for instance, although so far he hasn't bothered. But I don't think it will help the investigation much. One lance is very like another. But if you would like to see it, why don't you come up to the barracks? Tomorrow morning, say?'

'Monsieur Seymour!'
'*Cher collègue!*'
'Again you find me here!'
'And what better place to find you?' said Seymour. 'A Pernod, perhaps?'
Several Pernods later:
'And so, Monsieur Renaud, I come to you. Puzzled.'
'Puzzled?'
'If this had happened in England, that would have been the first thing I thought. A pretty woman, admirers, a husband in the way. The husband gets removed. Wrong, no doubt. But surprising? Not at all. What could be more natural?'
'Ah, yes, Monsieur, but –'
'A pretty woman, yes?'
'Oh, yes!' said Renaud fervently.
'Admirers?'
'Yes, but –'
'I have heard them, you have heard them. Young men, men of action, soldiers used to violence. Would it be surprising if –?'
'Well, no. But –'

171

'That is the first thing I would have thought. If I had been in England. And are things so different in Tangier?'

'Well, no, of course.'

'That is what a man of experience would have thought straightaway, surely? And Monsieur Renaud is a man of experience, I said to myself. Surely he has thought that? Of course he has, I said to myself! This will be the first thing he looked into. And what has he seen? That is the question I asked myself. What has Monsieur Renaud seen? And what is he not saying!'

'Well. Well . . .'

'Come, Monsieur Renaud. We are colleagues. We understand each other, yes? You have looked into this and found something, and now you are not saying! Isn't that true? Come, Monsieur Renaud!'

'Well . . .'

'Between ourselves.'

'Well . . .'

Renaud shifted uneasily.

'The fact is, Monsieur, I have found nothing.'

'Ah! You say that, but –'

'No, it is true. I did wonder when I first heard – heard that Bossu was dead. I didn't know the circumstances then, of course. It is true I did ask myself – but then I thought: no, it could not be, Juliette is spotless –'

'Spotless, Monsieur?'

'Yes, yes. It is true that she has her admirers –'

'Ah!'

'But she keeps them at a distance.'

'On a string?'

'Perhaps you could say that.'

'And perhaps one of them was not content with that?'

'Well, I don't think any of them liked it, but –'

He pulled himself together.

'It was just a game. For her, at any rate. She was perhaps a little bit of a flirt. Perhaps. No, definitely. But, then, she was a woman. And aren't all women like that? All French-women, at any rate.'

172

Monsieur Renaud hesitated.

'But perhaps not all Englishwomen? I do not know. I lack experience, alas. Personally, I have always found Englishwomen rather flat-chested. So perhaps they . . . But Frenchwomen –' gathering confidence now that he was on familiar ground – 'love to play. And Juliette is like that. Playful. She spreads her wings like . . . like a great, gorgeous butterfly –'

'Gosh, yes!' said Seymour.

'– and draws men to her.'

'Well, yes!' said Seymour. 'Of course! I can see that.'

'But it is just play. Innocent play. Deep down her heart was true.'

'Really?'

'Yes. True to Bossu. So there was never any question –'

'But, Monsieur Renaud, Bossu was often away. And in his absence –'

'It is true,' conceded Renaud, 'that in his absence Juliette may have spread her wings a little wider than usual.'

'And the officers came running.'

'Well, Monsieur, you have to understand how it is in Tangier. For young men. Young Frenchmen, that is. They are far from home. And there are a lot of them. Perhaps you have not sufficiently appreciated that, Monsieur Seymour. There are soldiers everywhere in Morocco. It is not like that in England, no?'

'No,' said Seymour.

There were soldiers in London, of course, and occasionally you saw them being thrown out of the public houses at closing time. But you didn't actually see them much otherwise.

'And perhaps not in France,' said Renaud. 'But here, in Morocco, it is different. There are soldiers everywhere. There have to be. This is not like France or England. It is a wild country, a frontier country. So there are soldiers everywhere. It is like one big garrison town. Lots of soldiers, but no women.

173

'No women, Monsieur Seymour! Can you appreciate that? I can, I was a young man myself once. So when a beautiful butterfly spreads its wings –'

'But, Monsieur Renaud, aren't you supporting everything I said?'

'No! No. For Juliette is not like that. She spreads her wings, but that is all. Giving her favours? No. If only,' he said sadly.

Behind him, as he walked back to the hotel, Mustapha and Idris were chatting.

'You'll see about the truck, then?'

'I will. When will we need it for?'

There was a pause.

'In about a week's time? I reckon it will all be over by then. Our friend here is increasingly looking like a dog that's found its bone. Give it ten days to be on the safe side.'

'Better not make it too long, Mustapha. I'm skint.'

'Me, too. The old woman keeps saying, "When are you getting back to work, Mustapha?" "When this job's done," I say. "This is a question of honour." "Honour doesn't buy the bread," she says. "And the children are beginning to complain." "They've got to learn," I say. "They've got to learn that honour comes first. You tell them that." "I do, Mustapha, I do," she says. "And that one day you'll be proud of them."'

'Quite right!' said Idris approvingly. 'Tell the little buggers!'

'"But," she says –'

'With women there's always a "but",' growled Idris.

'"But," she says, "there's another one on the way. And this is not a time to go short."'

'I hope it's a boy,' said Idris.

'Oh, bound to be,' Mustapha assured him. 'I will say this for Fatima, she's on a good run. Two boys already, and now probably a third. If she goes on like this, I could have a gang of my own. And then we'd be all right, wouldn't we, Idris? We'd have a bit of muscle.'

'We'd sort out bloody Ali Khadr,' said Idris.

'We would. And there's another thing – you don't mind if I say this, Idris? Isn't it about time you settled down yourself? I mean, it's all very well going to Mother Mina's, but doesn't there come a time when you're wasting your seed?'

'I have thought of that,' acknowledged Idris. 'The fact is, I've been waiting.'

'You can wait too long, you know, Idris.'

'Waiting to see if Khabradji's got one on the way this time. And, of course, if she has, we'll get married. Only I don't want to marry her if she's not – well, you need to be sure, don't you? Sure she can have children.'

'Well, there is that.'

'I've wondered if I ought to wait a bit longer even then. Just to make sure it's a boy.'

'Well, Idris, these things are in the hand of God, and once you know she can bear one, I wouldn't bother about the others. Even if the first is only a girl. I mean, she'll be on the right lines, won't she? And sooner or later it's bound to come right and you'll have a boy.'

There was a silence.

Then Idris said:

'I think, as a matter of fact, Mustapha, that there could be one on the way right now.'

'Well, that's very good. That's very good, Idris.'

'But Khabradji is saying: now I've got to do my bit.'

'But if one is on the way, haven't you done –'

'No, no, she means a house. And the things that go inside it. She's already made a list. "That's all very well," I say, "but it's all got to wait until I've made a hit." "Go on and make a hit, then," she says, "and don't take too long about it." So the fact is, the sooner we make a run, the better.'

'Yes, well, you go ahead and line up a truck. And then we can get started.'

175

A pause. Then –

'Mustapha?'

'Yes?'

'What are we going to put in it? On the down run, I mean?'

'Guns?'

'If it's going to be guns, we'll have to set that up.'

'I'll do that,' said Mustapha decisively.

'And ammunition,' said Idris.

'Of course.'

Another silence. Then –

'Mustapha?'

'Yes, Idris?'

'We'll need to take someone with us. We'll need a mechanic. Those pissing roads tear a truck apart.'

'Well, they do, Idris, if it's a truck like the last one you got.'

'You can't get better ones!' protested Idris. 'Not for our sort of money.'

'Of course you can!'

'No, you can't. You haven't been able to for some time now. First, because there are a lot of people running arms down now and they've got more money than we have. That Frenchman, for instance. The one our friend is interested in. Money no object! And then, besides, mechanics are not too keen these days. Not since that truck was blown up.'

'That was years ago!'

'I know. But it's the sort of thing people remember. Especially if they're a mechanic. Like the one who was killed.'

'Pay them more.'

'It's easy to say that, Mustapha, but if we're paying more for the truck as well . . .'

Another silence.

'Idris?'

'Yes, Mustapha?'

'The truck that was blown up: that was a very long time ago.'

'It was, Mustapha. But people remember it. Especially in times like the present.'

'I remember it,' said Mustapha, after a moment.

'And so do I,' said Idris. 'Bloody terrifying, wasn't it? We weren't that far behind. In fact, I thought for a moment that it was we that were goners, not him.'

'They must have put something in the road,' said Mustapha. 'Covered it over with sand.'

'I saw the bastards,' said Idris. 'They were lying down beside the road. That doesn't look right, I thought. They're up to something. Only I reckon the bloke in front didn't see it in time. Whoosh, it went!'

'I jumped on the brakes,' said Mustapha, 'and turned the truck. "Let's get to hell out of here," I said.'

'We don't want anything like that happening this time,' said Idris.

'We certainly don't!' said Mustapha fervently.

When Seymour came down to go out for a meal Chantale was working at her desk. He lingered, half hoping he might persuade her to come out with him.

'Can't!' she said. 'I've got to finish this.'

'More gossip?'

'It's something I've got to get to the printer's tonight.'

'Oh!' said Seymour, disappointed.

'It's for the boys.'

'The boys?'

'Sadiq and his friends. I promised Awad. It's a stunt they're up to and they want some publicity for it. I'm going to try the main newspapers but if they don't want it, I'll put it in *New Dawn*.'

'You write for *New Dawn*?'

'I write for anybody who'll print me.'

'Even if they can't pay you?'

'I have a soft spot for *New Dawn*. Their heart is in the

right place. Even if their head isn't. There are not many papers these days who stand up for Morocco. Old Morocco, I mean, not French Morocco. *New Dawn* is one of the few.'

'I'm surprised,' said Seymour. He hesitated. 'I would have thought *New Dawn* wasn't quite your line.'

'Why would you have thought that?'

'Difficult for you, I know. But I would have thought that perhaps your sympathies were with the French.'

Chantale pushed her writing away.

'I'm torn,' she said. 'On this as on everything. Half of me says Morocco is a backward place and the French will improve it. Particularly for women. The other half shrieks and says, "Don't do this to us!"'

'I can understand that.'

She toyed with her pencil.

'I gather you've met Benchennouf?'

'Yes. Sadiq took me to see him.'

'And what did you think of him?'

'Well . . .'

Chantale laughed.

'Yes,' she said. 'Well!'

'I was really interested in what he might have to tell me about Casablanca. At the time of the trouble. And about the part that Bossu played.'

'And what did he tell you?' Chantale asked.

'It was mostly about the part that *New Dawn* played.'

'Well, yes,' said Chantale. 'It would be.'

'Apparently *New Dawn* had got details of some contracts. Benchennouf said that it really enabled him to take the lid off.'

She seemed amused.

'If it did,' she said wryly, 'they very soon put it on again!'

'Yes. He said that *New Dawn* was suppressed and that he had to get out of Casablanca in a hurry. And so he was never quite able to make use of the information. That is, until recently.'

'Yes,' said Chantale. 'That's right.'

'But that when Bossu was appointed clerk to Macfarlane's committee he suddenly saw how he could make use of it.'

'"He" suddenly saw?' said Chantale. 'He wouldn't have seen it in a million years! I suggested it.'

'*You* suggested it?'

Chapter Twelve

'Perhaps,' said Chantale, 'I should tell you something. It is about my family; and in particular about my father. You may have heard something of this, but I want to tell you myself.

'My father was a soldier. He came from one of those military families in which for many generations the men have been soldiers. So it was natural for him to become one too. He went to military college, the best, and did very well. He won all sorts of honours and was chosen as the best cadet of his year. All sorts of things were predicted for him.

'When he graduated he was posted to Algeria, which he liked. It was where the action was and where there were chances to excel. Shortly after he arrived in Algeria he met my mother. They fell in love. Whatever my father did, he did passionately. And so he fell passionately in love. But there was, of course, a complication. My mother wasn't French. She was Moroccan. Not Algerian, you understand? She just happened to be visiting. She had relations in Algiers. There were three sisters and they were all beautiful and so there were always officers visiting the house. It wasn't common, but the family was well to do and European in its ways. And one day my mother met my father.

'I told you that my father was passionate. He wanted to marry her. My mother's relations were aghast, and so was his family back in France. It wasn't done, you understand? They wanted her to marry a decent young Muslim, Moroccan, preferably, but Algerian would do. But my father persuaded them. Or perhaps he didn't persuade them, perhaps he just went ahead and did it. He was like that. It was the way he was.

'Of course, his family back in France did not like it and I think there was a rupture. He never spoke of his family afterwards.

'And the army didn't like it, either. They posted him all over the place, to the wildest parts, where there was always fighting. But it did give him the chance to excel. He was promoted and promoted. But all the time there was my mother. And then me. You have heard about all this, perhaps? People talk, I know.'

'I have heard something, yes,' said Seymour.

'Well,' she said, 'I have grown used to it. But let me move on to Casablanca. And to Bossu. There came a time when French troops were sent to Morocco, and my father went with them. He was pleased because he thought he would be able to spend more time with my mother. And he hardly knew me.

'One day he was sent to Casablanca. There had been trouble there. You probably know about this. They were developing the sea front and for the new buildings they required stone. There was a suitable quarry not far away and some businessmen built a railway line from it to where the building was going on. Unfortunately, they ran it through a Muslim cemetery. It didn't matter to them, I suppose they thought they could buy their way out of it. But the Muslims erupted. They attacked the men working on the railway line and killed some of them.

'The authorities sent in troops to put down what they saw as a riot. Some of the Muslims were killed and that, of course, led to more riots. The disorder spread, and more troops were sent in. Among them was my father.

'The soldiers suppressed the rioting. Very bloodily. And one day my father objected. He said he was a soldier and that his job was to fight soldiers and not massacre civilians.

181

Quite a lot of the soldiers felt as he did and there was, for a time, for a day or two, a pause.

'But then the city authorities and the businessmen complained. They asked what was the army doing? And, of course, they had influence back in Tangier, and back in France, too, so the fighting resumed.

'But my father refused. He said that the orders were wrong and that he would not obey them. The Casablanca authorities wanted him tried for mutiny. But the army knew it couldn't do that because so many of the officers agreed with him. And even if they didn't agree, they respected him. He was a very good soldier and popular throughout the army.

'In the end he was persuaded that the honourable thing to do was to resign his commission. He left the army and tried to make a life as a civilian. That wasn't easy. He tried being a farmer but that didn't work out. Nothing seemed to work out. And it was only slowly that we understood why.

'The settlers hadn't forgotten what he had done and were hostile. But it went further than that. There seemed to be some sort of campaign against him. Wherever he went, whatever he tried, things went wrong. And gradually we realized that this wasn't an accident. Somebody was organizing it.

'As first we couldn't believe it. But then one day someone told us.

'The person who was organizing it was Bossu. Again we couldn't believe it. My father had come up against him in Casablanca and, yes, he had sensed his hostility. But he couldn't believe that he would carry it so far. Carry it on after he had left Casablanca and so long after he had left Casablanca. But so it appeared to be.

'And it went on. It began to colour everything we did. We realized that they wanted us out – out of Morocco altogether. But my mother was Moroccan! And my father was not the man to give in. He said that he had made up his mind to make a life here and make a life he would.

'Well, in the end he was killed in a road accident. That was terrible. I was very young at the time and I thought the world had fallen apart. It was very hard for us, for my mother, perhaps, especially. We had to make our way alone. But we thought that at least the relentless persecution would stop.

'But it didn't. It seemed to pursue us, whatever we did. We tried various things and again they did not work out. And, again, people told us it was not by accident.

'So we decided to move back to here, where we were known, and where perhaps people would protect us. Friends helped us buy the hotel. And then, the first day, the hotel was broken up! It may have been chance but, with our experience, we thought it unlikely. Friends told us that it was Bossu.

'Well, then it stopped, and we thought that perhaps he had finally decided to make an end of it. But I did not forget it. And when he was appointed Secretary to the committee, I thought the chance had come to get my own back. I put into Benchennouf's head the idea that now was the time to stir old memories, to remind people about Casablanca and what Bossu had done there. I even wrote some of the articles. And if it worked, if it did stir old feelings, and if, because of that, someone killed Bossu, then I am glad.'

When Seymour left the hotel to go out to dinner, usually either Mustapha or Idris was waiting there to accompany him. This time they both were, and with them were two other men who had plainly just arrived.

'Mustapha,' one of them said, 'I don't know why I come to you.'

Mustapha looked surprised.

'Hello, Fazal,' said Idris.

And now Seymour remembered the man. It was the elusive carter. The man with the shifting apartment and the shifting wife, whom Idris had so industriously finally tracked down to the stables.

'Hello, Fazal,' said Seymour.

The man gave a slight bow of acknowledgement and then looked him straight in the face.

'It is chiefly for you, Monsieur, that I have come. For I think you are an honest man. Unlike these two.'

'Here, watch it –' began Mustapha and Idris together.

'Why you should be so interested in the death of the fat Frenchman I do not know. It is said that you are a policeman. But in my experience policemen do not usually concern themselves greatly with such matters. At least in Morocco. Perhaps it is because you do not come from Tangier and do not know the way things are done.

'And how you should have met up with Mustapha and Idris I do not know, either. It seems unexpected to me. It is said they are your bodyguard, and certainly you need one if you go on like this. But to choose Mustapha and Idris! Monsieur, let me counsel you. You could do better.'

'Fazal, are you trying to make trouble?'

'I am not afraid of your knife, Mustapha. At least, not when there are witnesses about. It is just that I am puzzled. Takings, I can see, must have dropped off, but –'

'This, Fazal, is a question of honour!'

'Oh, I see –'

'No, you don't, Fazal. It is not a matter of money. Our friend stood up for me when Ali Khadr came. Should I not stand for him?'

'Unquestionably you should. But –'

'I am hurt, Fazal, that you should question me on a point of honour.'

'Fazal –' began Fazal's companion nervously.

'And offended.'

'Fazal –'

'Oh, I am not questioning,' said Fazal hastily. 'Not on a point of honour. Not in any way. I am just surprised, that's all.'

'Well, just contain your surprise,' said Idris.

'Who is this bloke, anyway?' demanded Mustapha, looking at Fazal's companion.

'He is my friend. Fuad, his name is. And I bring him to the Monsieur because I said I would. I, too, Mustapha, have a sense of honour!'

'Ah!' said Seymour. 'This is the friend who was with you on the day of the pig-sticking. The day the Frenchman was killed?'

'That is so, yes, Monsieur. I said that perhaps there were things that his eye had seen and that mine had missed.'

'That is always possible. Thank you, Fazal, for bringing me your friend. And thank you, Fuad, for agreeing to come.'

'I wouldn't have come,' said Fuad, 'had Fazal not pressed me.'

'I am glad that he did. And was it so? Did your eye see something that his had missed?'

The first part of the story was familiar ground but Seymour took him through it.

'And are you sure, Fuad,' he said at the end of Fuad's recital, 'that there were two horses?'

'Positive, Monsieur. One ran off ahead of us. And that, I think, must have been the Frenchman's horse, for it was riderless.'

'And the other?'

'Rode the other way, back the way we had come.'

'To rejoin the hunt?'

'I think so, Monsieur. For the rider was holding a lance. But, Effendi . . .'

'Yes?'

'Afterwards, I was puzzled. For I had taken the man for one of Musa's men. But how could that be, if he was carrying a lance?'

'Why did you take him for one of Musa's men?'

'I did not see him clearly, Effendi. I lost him almost at

once in the scrub. But he stopped for a moment to disentangle his headdress from the thorn, so I thought –'

'Monsieur Ricard –'

Monsieur Ricard surveyed him with a baleful but, possibly surprisingly for that hour in the morning, recognizing eye.

'The Englishman!'

'Just so. And, like you, I suspect, getting ready for the pig-sticking tomorrow.'

'I don't need to get ready,' growled Monsieur Ricard. 'I am always ready.'

'A little practice, perhaps?'

'Practice! I don't need practice. When you've been pig-sticking as long as I have . . . No, all I shall do today is see that the horse is all right. In so far as it will ever be all right! I need a new one.'

'I think you mentioned that.'

'One which will keep up. This one is too old. "Like you, Father," my daughter says. The idiot! What does she know about it?'

'You are as old as you feel, Monsieur, and you, obviously, feel in the best of health.'

'I do. And I don't need that idiot, Millet, telling me otherwise.'

'You are looking forward to the event tomorrow?'

'Certainly.'

'I wish you well, Monsieur Ricard. It was a great pleasure to visit you the other day and benefit from your knowledge. Not just of pig-sticking but also of Tangier.'

'I should know it. I've been here a long time.'

'Then you, perhaps, are the very person who can help me over something that's been puzzling me. When you spoke so interestingly about the young Bossu and what lay behind his marriage to the charming Juliette, you said that the marriage had nearly not come about because of one of Bossu's previous affairs. A most unsuitable affair, you said.

186

Certainly, from what you told me, her family appeared to view it so.'

'He wanted to *marry her*. That was the unsuitable bit. As an affair, there was nothing wrong with it. Lots of young men have affairs with Moroccans. But when you start talking about marriage –'

'She was a Moroccan?'

'Very much so. And the family couldn't have that. It was one of the older settler families. French through and through. It would have been a blot. Even though it was in the past. People would always have been saying that Juliette was second choice after a Moroccan! Well!'

He gave one of his old-man laughs.

'Of course, in the end they did accept him. In the end, money talked loudest. It usually does, doesn't it? Bossu had the money, so in the end he had the girl.'

He started to laugh again, then stopped.

'Mind you, it didn't work that way with the other one. She turned him down. I'll bet that was a shock! Turned down by a Moroccan! She wouldn't have anything to do with him.'

'And the name of this lady was . . .?'

'Do they have names?' Ricard laughed.

The laugh turned into a frown.

'I used to know it once. I forget everything these days. Marie, was it? Something like that. Anyway, I can tell you who she was. The mother of that . . .' He had to search again. '. . . Chantale!' he shouted triumphantly.

The barracks was on the edge of town. It was surrounded by a perimeter fence and outside the fence was a bare, sandy area where, to judge by the condition of the sand, horses were exercised. Inside the fence was a large square where men might parade and recruits be given foot drill, and, beyond that, a number of low single-storey buildings. Seymour gave his name at the gate and asked to see

Captain de Grassac. An orderly was sent off and soon de Grassac himself appeared.

They shook hands.

'You have come to see the lance? It won't take long. There's nothing very special about it, I'm afraid. But then you can come into the Mess and we'll have something.'

He took Seymour behind the main building and then into another building where the officers had their quarters. He opened a door and led Seymour into a surprisingly comfortable room lined with books.

De Grassac waved a hand at them almost apologetically.

'One gets into the way of reading out in the outposts,' he said. 'There is not a lot else one can do.'

He went through an inner door and emerged carrying a lance, which he gave to Seymour.

Seymour turned it over in his hands.

'Where do people get lances from?' he asked.

'There's a place in the city you can buy them from. Darquier's. This was probably bought there, but I don't know that will help you.'

He took the lance and turned it over almost fondly.

'This is obviously an Old Faithful,' he said, 'and was bought some time ago. I doubt if their records will show anything.'

'Mind if I keep it for a day or two?'

'Not at all.'

He looked at his watch.

'The bar will be open. Would you like to see our Mess?'

He took Seymour into another building where officers were gathering, and then looked at Seymour inquiringly.

'We usually drink beer at this time,' he said, 'to replace the liquid we sweat out during training.'

'Beer will do fine.'

De Grassac returned with two beers and sat down.

'How are you getting on with your investigation?'

'Nearly there, I think.'

De Grassac raised his eyebrows.

'Really?' he said. 'You surprise me.'

'There are still one or two things to tie up. I'm still learning things about Bossu. As a man. He doesn't seem to have been very nice. If what Chantale says about him is true.'

'You've been talking to Chantale? No, he was not a nice man.'

'I can understand Bossu's animosity towards de Lissac when they were in Casablanca. It was a time when feelings ran high. And Bossu had put a lot into building the railway. Of himself, I mean. It was one of his first projects and he wanted it to succeed. And he felt he hadn't started too well, either. With all the trouble. And then de Lissac came along and made things worse. I can understand Bossu feeling angry. But what I can't understand is why his anger should continue afterwards. If it did.'

'Oh, it did.'

'Why was that, do you think?'

De Grassac shrugged.

'Maybe because of the kind of man Bossu was?' he offered.

'I wondered if there was some previous history between them?'

'Not as far as I know.'

'You were at the wedding, if I remember. Of de Lissac and Chantale's mother. Was there anything there?'

'I don't think so.'

'Involving Bossu?'

'It seems unlikely. Wasn't he in Tangier?'

'I just wondered if something had come up.'

'Not as far as I can recall. You remember it was, well, a private wedding. Rather in secret. There weren't many people there.'

'No, but I wondered if you had picked something up.'

'Look,' said de Grassac, 'I wasn't there long enough to pick *anything* up. I had been in a fort on the other side of Algeria. I had come over especially for the wedding. Because de Lissac asked me to. I had got a leave pass for fifty-six hours and then I had to be back. I spent most of the time travelling.'

'Okay, but there *was* something. I wondered if you had picked it up. If not then, perhaps later.'

De Grassac was silent, for quite a long time.

'Perhaps,' he said.

'You see, it might account for the animosity.'

De Grassac said nothing.

'Did it?' said Seymour.

De Grassac was silent for quite a while. Then he said:

'Chantale, at any rate, thought it did. She even – she thought Bossu might have had a hand in her father's death.'

He looked at Seymour.

'You know about this?'

'Only that he had died. In some kind of road accident.'

'She wondered if it *was* an accident. She asked me to go down and see. She couldn't go herself, she was still at school, I think, and, anyway, a woman down there, on her own – it was out of the question. So I got leave and went down there. He had been driving a truck. Full of explosives.'

'Explosives?'

'Yes. It was for some contractors building a road. They needed the dynamite to blast rocks. It was quite legitimate. I checked. I talked to the contractor. The thing was, you see, that they needed someone they could rely on to deliver the dynamite. There were bandits down there and explosives are much sought after. You had to have someone you could trust. And the fact that Marcel had been an army officer was a help – he knew about explosives and wouldn't be stupid. And Marcel, I think, needed the work.'

He shrugged.

'Well, there was an explosion, and Marcel was killed. It seems to have been a genuine accident. I checked as much as I could. There were no eyewitnesses, unfortunately, or if there were, they made themselves scarce, as eyewitnesses

190

do down there. I checked as much as I could but couldn't find anything which suggested that it wasn't an accident. And an accident was quite likely. Bumpy roads, not even a road, actually, just a track. Dynamite is always dangerous to handle. In the end I had to go back and tell Chantale that it *was* an accident.'

'Was there anyone else in the truck? Killed with him?'

'A mechanic, I think.'

'So where are you off to?' asked Mrs Macfarlane.

He had met her on the sea front, off, she said, to pick up her husband for lunch.

'On my way to a tailor's,' said Seymour.

'You are having something made up?'

'A suit. He's done one for me already and it was so good that I thought I would have another done while I was here.'

'You couldn't do better. The work is always so good. And the prices are very reasonable.' She hesitated. 'You, of course, know about prices here. And about God's door?'

'God's door?'

'Well, you know there is no such thing as a fixed price out here. To put a price on a thing without a human exchange seems to a Moroccan the height of vulgarity. It goes along with the *caida*, I suppose. So you have to negotiate everything. But even when you do, you always leave a little leeway so that if something doesn't turn out as you expected, the coat needs more doing to it than you had thought, for example, you always have room to adjust. That's God's door. A way out. And Moroccans always like to leave it open.'

'What is it this time, then?' asked Idris, just before they went into the shop. 'Another suit? Believe me, you couldn't do better.'

Ali, the tailor, came forward anxiously.

'There is no problem, I hope? It fits you well, surely?'
'It fits me perfectly.'
Ali looked relieved.
'A simple cleaning up? More blood, perhaps?'
'More blood?' said Mustapha. 'What do you take us for? We're looking after him.'
'It was your blood last time,' Ali pointed out.
'Ah, well, that was different. It was before we were looking after him. And, anyway, it was one of Ali Khadr's little games.'
'I thought he was supposed to be coming round again? Last night, was it? Or is it tonight?'
'He's not coming,' said Idris disgustedly.
'Someone stopped it,' said Mustapha.
'Chantale's mother,' said Idris.
'And very sensible of her,' said Ali. He looked at Seymour. 'Then what can I do for you, Monsieur?'
'Another suit, please. Exactly like the other. The same fit. But different material.'
'Easy!' said Ali.
'And some information,' said Seymour.
'Information?'
'I remember that you told me once, the first time I came, I think, that Bossu had been one of your customers.'
'That is true. But it was a long time ago. A long, long time ago. When he first arrived in Tangier. He was a poor man then. That, perhaps, was why he came to me. Also, he lived here.'
'Here?'
'Just around the corner. He was, as I say, a poor man then.'
'So he knew the neighbourhood?'
'Yes.'
'And the people?'
'Of course.'
'Including Chantale's mother?'
'He knew the family. The father worked in the Mahzen. Not a high post but a respectable one. And the family was

192

a respectable one, too. Well-to-do, decent. So he would not have met Chantale's mother. Things were different in those days. She was kept hidden. And behind a veil. So he should never have seen her. But somehow he did.

'The mother used to come to me sometimes when she wanted work done. And once she came with her daughter. Bossu must have seen them because afterwards he came to me and said, "Who is that beautiful girl?" And I said, "I do not know." Because I had never seen her without a veil. But Bossu said, "She is with her mother." "Well, yes," I said, "and she should be." "What is her mother's name, then?" Perhaps I should not have told him, but I did.

'He went away and I thought no more about it. But then one day I heard he had been to the father and asked for his daughter's hand. By this time Bossu was growing wealthy and it would have been a good match. Except that he was a Frenchman! "Ill will come of this!" said the family, and they refused him.

'But Bossu had friends in the Mahzen and someone must have spoken to the father, for he was allowed to renew his suit. But this time it was she who refused. The father might now have said, "Peace! The man has powerful friends." But the mother said, "No, she doesn't want him." So they sent her away to relations in Algeria, and that should have been the end of it.

'And so for a time it was. But then we heard that he had followed her to Algeria and importuned her there. Only things were looser there. The family allowed her to mix with people and show her face. And now there were other men who admired her and sought her hand.

'One, in particular: a young Frenchman. And her relatives said, "This is getting serious." And they wrote to her father and told him. And he said, "Send her back." And she was to have gone. But she knew that she could be returning not just to her family but also to Bossu. And one day we heard that she had fled with her young officer.

'Her family cast her out. And when she returned to Tangier, it was years later and her parents were dead. And she came as a married woman with a child. Her husband was much away and in another country. But this was where she had friends and so she came back here and lived among us until her husband was sent to Morocco. But by that time Bossu was gone and we heard no more of him.'

Chapter Thirteen

As Seymour came out of the shop he felt his arm seized.

'Why, Monsieur Seymour!' cooed the soft voice of Juliette Bossu. 'Are you out shopping, too?'

'Well, not exactly.'

'What is that thing you are carrying? Surely not a lance?'

'A souvenir of Morocco. To take home to my mother.'

'A lance?' said Juliette doubtfully. But then put Seymour's concerns aside.

'I made Constant bring me. I always feel safer with a man, you know, especially these days when it is so easy for a lone woman to be attacked. But, do you know what, the wretch has deserted me!'

Juliette sighed theatrically.

'But when duty calls, I suppose a man has to go. Someone came running up and told him, and the dear man felt he should be there. "But what about me, Constant?" I cried. "Do you not also have a duty to me? Am I to be left alone to be ravished in the street?" Alone, that was, Monsieur Seymour,' said Madame Bossu fondly, 'until I met you!'

'Well, yes, Madame. Thank you. Yes. I'm sure – you will be quite safe with me – although I *was* going –'

'Oh, thank you!' breathed Juliette. 'And now let us go and have a nice tête-à-tête over coffee. Just the two of us, I know the very place!' She thrust her arm firmly through Seymour's.

'Well, thank you. Yes, that would be nice. Very nice. But – what about Monsieur Renaud? Should he return?'

'Oh, he will know where to find me. Anyway he shouldn't have abandoned me. Suppose they come down the street and fall upon me?'

'Indeed. Yes, indeed! But – who, exactly, Madame, might fall upon you?'

'They, of course! The students!'

'The students?'

'Have you not heard? They have risen in revolt. And seized the main madrassa block! And they have closed the classes, and hung dreadful banners from the windows and are shouting the most awful things!'

'No, I hadn't –'

But now, in the distance, he could hear shouting and chanting, and he suddenly remembered what Chantale had said about the students planning some 'stunt'.

'I don't think you need to be too alarmed,' he said.

'But, Monsieur Seymour, you do not know these people! They are not like us. Excitement goes to their head and they become violent. There is talk of a procession, and it might come down here, and then what will we do?'

'Well, what we could do, Madame, is follow your excellent suggestion and go for some refreshment.'

'Well, we could. I suppose . . .'

She led him across the street and into a small *salon de thé*.

'And we could watch the procession as it passes!' said Juliette happily. 'I do love a procession! A peaceful one, of course. They usually have bands. But –' Her face clouded over. 'The way they dress! So drab! There is no style, Monsieur Seymour, no style! If they would just spend a few moments with me, I could – But, perhaps, on second thoughts, that might not be a good idea. They have no respect, that is the problem. That is what I said to Monsieur Renaud. "Too right!" he said. "And that is just what I am going to teach them!" And then he went off and left me –'

'You are quite safe now, Madame.'

He looked covertly at his watch. A quick cup of tea and then he might get rid of her.

'Although I would not wish to take you from your shopping –'

'Oh, you won't! I have done most of it.'

'Well, then, we can enjoy our tea.'

Fortunately, they did not have to enjoy it for long. The face of Monsieur Renaud appeared round the door.

'Juliette!'

'Constant!' said Madame Bossu, not altogether pleased.

'You are safe?'

'I am safe. With Monsieur Seymour,' she said pointedly.

'Do, please, join us, Monsieur Renaud,' said Seymour hastily.

'I may?'

He pulled up a chair.

'And you, too, are safe, Constant,' said Juliette, relenting slightly.

'It was nothing.'

'I hope you did not risk yourself, Constant. Those *sauvages*!'

'It was nothing. I put a picquet on. A few policemen. The students shouted, of course. Jeered.'

'The brutes!'

'But you expect that from students these days. Now in my day –'

Juliette cut him short.

'Have you arrested them?'

'Well, no –'

'But why not?'

'Juliette, there are hundreds of them! And I only have half a dozen policemen!'

'Why have you not sent for the army?'

'Well, of course, it could come to that –'

'You should assert yourself, Constant. Crush them. That way they learn.'

'Yes, well –'

197

'You are too soft. The only language they understand is bullets.'

'Bullets, Juliette?'

'Well, why not?'

'Well, one reason is that the newspapers were there –'

'The newspapers? But surely Monsieur Lambert can take care of those?'

'Yes, but –' Renaud wriggled. 'Some of them were foreign, Juliette. Spanish, English –'

'We should expel them!'

'But even then, Juliette. Word would get out. You have no idea – It is very difficult –'

'It is always difficult, Constant. For you,' said Madame Bossu. 'But you must be resolute. What does it matter if word does get out? They expect you to be firm, Constant. They are only students, after all.'

'Yes, but – some of the newspaper men were inside the building. Talking to the students.'

'Well?'

'Getting their point of view.'

'So?'

'Mademoiselle Chantale, for instance –'

'That woman!' Juliette cried. 'But she is a *sauvage* herself! She attacked a woman in the street. Poor Madame Poiret. She struck her, actually struck her!'

'Juliette, calm yourself –'

'No, Constant. I will not. That woman is always causing trouble. She and her father. Yes, her father, too! As you know better than anyone.'

'Juliette, really –'

'He quarrelled with everyone! Even with poor Bossu!'

'Juliette –'

'When he was only trying to help him.'

'Help him?' asked Seymour.

She turned on him.

'Yes,' she said. 'You don't know this, do you? You only hear one side. It is always: de Lissac good, so good, Bossu bad. But it was not like that. Yes, they were against each other in Casablanca, and bitter things were said. But after-wards – when they were so poor. Destitute. When no one would help them. Bossu did what he could for them. He found de Lissac work. Yes! When no one else would. He got him a job. Driving a truck. "I know it's not much," he said, "but it's something. It will put you back on your feet. After that it's up to you. I know you don't like me. I don't like you. I'm doing it not for your sake but for hers." That's what he said. I heard him. When he came round to our house that morning. "It's a chance," Bossu said. "Take it or leave it. But it's meant well."'

'Juliette,' said Renaud, 'we don't need to go into this –'

'I know what they say about Bossu. That he had it in for him. But he didn't. It's not true. He helped him when no one else would. And as for the daughter! Stirring up trouble with the students. That's her, all right. Showing herself in her true colours. A troublemaker! Just like her father!'

Renaud finished his tea quickly and then said he must return to the students. Seymour, to Juliette's chagrin, said that he would go with him. He could still hear the shouting in the distance and as they drew nearer, it grew louder.

'The idiots!' said Renaud. 'The last thing that Tangier needs just at the moment is this sort of thing.'

'It is to be expected, I suppose,' said Seymour. 'With the French moving in. You're lucky you've not had it before.'

'It will do no good,' said Renaud.

'Of course not! But sometimes it is desirable to let feelings be expressed.'

Renaud was silent. Then he said:

'As long as it doesn't get out of hand.'

'A few students?'

'It could spread. I've seen this sort of thing before. A few people. You think it is nothing. But then suddenly other people are drawn in, and the next moment it is spreading like wildfire. And the moment after that the whole town is ablaze. I've seen it, Monsieur Seymour, I've seen it. You don't know these people. Volatile. Excitable. You've got to stop it before it catches fire.'

'Let them shout their heads off for a bit,' advised Seymour. 'And then have a word with them. Tell them to go home.'

'But while they're shouting, others will be hearing.'

'Make sure they stay in the building. And then it doesn't matter if anyone does hear them.'

'But suppose they run out? I only have a few police-men –'

'Go in and talk to them, then. Tell them they've made their point. You've let them do that. Now it's time to go home.'

'But will they listen to me? Suppose they don't?'

'They'll listen to you if you talk to them in the right way.'

'They'd listen a lot more if I had a few soldiers here!' said Renaud, glancing around nervously.

The students had occupied a large block of the college and festooned it with banners. Students were leaning out of windows and shouting slogans. As Seymour listened, a chant began. Soon they were all joining in. Seymour didn't need to understand the words. Something like 'French out!' presumably.

Renaud left him and went to talk to some of his policemen.

Awad appeared at a door.

'This is a free zone,' he declared. 'A free Moroccan zone!'

'Now, lads –' began Renaud.

He was greeted with a chorus of jeers.

'Come on, lads, this won't do! You've got to stop it. You've got to go home.'

More jeers.

'Never!' said Awad. 'We shall not go home until Morocco is free!'

Now there were cheers as well as jeers.

'You see?' said Renaud, retreating.

Seymour saw Chantale standing at a door down the side of the building. She was surrounded by students and was writing furiously.

He walked round to her.

'How's the occupation going?'

'It's making its point, don't you think?' asked Chantale.

'That rather depends on what's said in the newspapers.'

'Alas,' said Chantale, 'I'm the only newspaper.'

'I thought there were dozens of you? Spanish, French, English –'

'That's what I told them,' said Chantale. 'It looked as if they were going to try beating up the students otherwise.'

'Are they going to go home when it gets dark?'

'This is the last day of Ramadan. Tonight everyone will break their fast. Usually they have a splendid feast. I don't think the students will want to miss that.'

Some more students came up and buttonholed her.

Sadiq came out of the door, saw Seymour and went up to him.

'Brilliant, isn't it?'

'Fantastic! I congratulate you.'

Sadiq looked around.

'I rather expected Benchennouf to be here,' he said. 'We told him what we were going to do and he was very pleased. "The revolution starts here!" he said. So we rather expected him to come. But I don't see him, do you?'

Awad joined them.

'I expected more people to be here!' he said, vexed. 'I expected ordinary people to rise up and join us!'

A small group of Moroccan officials had appeared at the end of the street.

'Ah! There's my father!' said Awad, and ran back inside.

A moment later he thrust his head through an open upper window and began shouting. Others joined him.

Renaud was talking to Suleiman Fazi.

'It's getting out of hand,' he said. 'We ought to act now.'

'Well, go on: act!' said Suleiman Fazi.

Renaud looked around.

'I've not got enough men,' he said. 'I need some soldiers.'

'Not soldiers!' said Suleiman Fazi.

'Soldiers,' muttered Renaud, preoccupied, and hurried away.

'Don't let him!' said Seymour.

Suleiman Fazi shrugged.

'I can't stop him,' he said. 'Can't do anything. I'm just the Minister.'

Chantale had been listening.

'Tell him to stop!' she said urgently. 'They're not really doing anything. Just shouting.'

'He won't listen to me. Nor will the French.'

'They'll listen to *me*!' said Chantale and hurried away.

Seymour walked over to the students.

'Can I talk to Awad?' he said.

'Why are you carrying that lance?'

'It's a souvenir. To remind me of Morocco.'

Someone went to fetch Awad.

'Congratulations!' said Seymour. 'You've done very well. Brilliantly. As good an occupation as I've seen! And, believe me, I've seen some.'

'In England?' said Awad, pleased.

'And in Istanbul,' said Seymour, stretching a point.

'Well!' said Awad, beaming. 'Well!'

'You won't mind if I suggest something? The trouble is with demonstrations that they usually fizzle out and the whole point is lost. People drift away. Don't let them. End by triumphantly marching off. You've made your point. You've made it brilliantly. Now disappear and leave them gaping!'

Awad looked thoughtful.

'Do you know,' he said, 'the mosque is saying something rather like that, too. They say this is Ramadan and we ought to behave ourselves. This is a holy festival and we ought not to have arranged our demonstration for during it.'

'Well, look,' said Seymour, 'you can put that right, can't you? Take yourselves off and say that you are doing it to ensure that Ramadan ends in the right way.'

'I went in to see him,' complained Renaud indignantly, 'and he turned me away! "Do your own dirty work!" he said. Well! It wasn't like this in the old days, I can tell you! "Do your own dirty work." I'm doing *his* dirty work. What can I do with a handful of policemen in a city of this size? When there is an emergency on this scale.'

'Nothing, *cher collègue*! Nothing.'

'I've a good mind to wash my hands of the whole affair.'

'Why not?'

'Well, one feels . . . one feels . . .'

'Responsible?' suggested Seymour.

'Exactly. Responsible. Somehow.'

'*Collègue*, they are talking of withdrawing by this evening.'

'They are?'

'It appears so.'

'Well . . . Well, that puts a different complexion on things.'

'If I were you,' said Seymour, 'I'd pull back your men to the end of the street. Or even into the next street. Where they'd be ready if needed but not too conspicuous. So as not to be too provocative. It would be foolish at this stage to provoke an incident, wouldn't it?'

'It certainly would!' said Renaud, much relieved. He went off to give the necessary orders.

'What can I do?' asked Suleiman Fazi.

'Congratulate Awad on the sense of responsibility he's

shown and on his zeal to stand up for freedom. And then ask him if he's coming home to share the Ramadan meal with you.'

'I will,' said the Vizier. 'I will!' and he walked forward to speak to the insurgents.

'All right?' Seymour asked Chantale, as she appeared round the corner.

'All right,' said Chantale. 'Lambert said the army was not to be used for every little incident. Besides, he doesn't like Renaud.'

'Why did he let them get away with the raid on the hotel?' asked Seymour.

Chantale looked at him, surprised.

'He was new in the job,' she said, 'and hadn't yet picked up the pieces.'

'Did he know the hotel belonged to you?'

'Of course. He'd been in the army here. They had gone to him when they found out . . . when they found out about us. It was Armand de Grassac's doing. He'd been away and then he came back and found that – well, we weren't doing too well. So he and the other officers talked to Lambert and money was found, somehow, I don't know how, but the money actually came from the army coffers, to help us buy the hotel. The Lamberts had always been kind to us. They made it possible for me to go to a French school. But he had only just been made Resident-General Designate and hadn't yet got everything in his hands.'

Seymour took Renaud by the arm and said: '*Collègue*, may I take a little walk with you?'

Renaud was still grumbling about Lambert.

'If I were you, *cher collègue*,' said Seymour, 'I would give the army a wide berth for a while.'

'Why so?'

'Because they provided the money for Chantale and her mother to buy the hotel. And I think they may be about to find out who tipped Ali Khadr off that the time had come to wreck it.'

Renaud went still.

'Perhaps even set the attack up. Who knows? But I think that if pressed Ali Khadr will tell them. There's quite a strong network in the quarter, which embraces the mosque and other influential people, and word gets around, you know, and I think that if it were put to Ali Khadr himself, well, you know, I think he would come clean. And if he did, *cher collègue*, I don't see how you could go on being Chief of Police in Tangier.'

Renaud remained mute.

'Even with powerful friends,' said Seymour.

'They will look after me,' muttered Renaud.

'You reckon? You know, colleague, I think they're the sort of people who would drop you in a flash if they thought it necessary. Despite everything you've done for them.'

'I have done nothing –'

'Oh? Well, let's start with Bossu. He was the man behind the raid on the hotel, wasn't he? And you were helping him, as you had always helped him. I suppose you were the first to find out that Chantale and her mother had bought the hotel and told him. And then he asked you to arrange a welcome party. Or perhaps he arranged it and merely asked you to tip off Ali Khadr when the time was ripe.'

'You cannot prove this –'

'No? Let us go on. With your knowledge of Bossu, Monsieur Renaud, perhaps you can tell me why his animosity towards the de Lissac family was such that he pursued Chantale and her mother, even after Captain de Lissac was dead? No? Well, let me tell you.

'I take it that you know about the passion that Bossu had originally felt for Marie de Lissac. And about how he had asked her to marry him. And been turned down. And then turned down again when he had pursued her to Algiers. I don't think he ever forgave that turning down. He was a man who always liked to win. And didn't like losing. Certainly not to de Lissac.

'It must have been a huge shock to him when de Lissac turned up in Casablanca. Especially when he began making himself a nuisance. But you were there, Monsieur Renaud, and would know. Would know, too, about how he then began to work systematically for de Lissac's destruction. A popular pursuit in Casablanca at the time, and he soon had plenty of people egging him on. Was that when you first made their acquaintance, *cher collègue*, and began to have an eye for their interests? Such an eye that it led to you becoming Chief of Police in Tangier?

'Well, there are other questions. Was it their interests that Bossu was following when he began taking money down to Moulay Hafiz and his supporters in the interior of Morocco? Opening up the interior. Building the railway line which would make possible the development of all that part of the country. Perhaps you don't know much about all that. That was Bossu's job, not yours.

'But there is one thing that you *do* know about and perhaps you can help me on. You see, I know that you know about it. Because Juliette Bossu obligingly blurted it out. It is to do with the death of Chantale's father, that long-standing enemy, as he saw it, of Bossu. Bossu persuaded him to drive a truck down to the south. A truck loaded with explosives to Moulay Hafiz. And on the way the truck exploded and Captain de Lissac was killed.'

'An accident,' muttered Monsieur Renaud.

'Ah, no.'

'It was investigated.'

'By you?'

'No, by – by the authorities.'

'The authorities? Down there?'

He waited.

'Does that mean Moulay Hafiz? Come on, Renaud, this is something I want to know.'

'It – it may have been. But – but there were others . . . Captain de Grassac . . . An independent . . .'

'Not a policeman, though, Renaud. Not a detective. Like you and me. I have investigated it, too. And I have found out things that Captain de Grassac didn't. Including that it was not an accident.'

'I – I don't know anything about it. Bossu handled it. Entirely, I mean. He didn't tell me anything. It is not the sort of thing that I would –'

'No, you wouldn't, Renaud. You'd leave that to others.'

When Seymour went into the hotel Chantale raised her head from her writing and said:

'Are you doing anything this evening? My mother wonders if you would care to join us for the evening meal. It is, of course, a special one, for it marks the end of Ramadan.'

Seymour said he would be delighted, and at about nine went down to reception, where he found the desk occupied by a polite young man whom he had not seen before. He rose from the desk, tapped softly on the door which led to the family's private quarters, and showed Seymour through.

Chantale came forward to greet him and led him out on to a small verandah where there was a low table spread for dinner with a white tablecloth. Around it were several large leather cushions. Chantale sat on one and invited him to sit next to her. Her mother appeared shortly after with a tray on which there were several small bowls, which she put on the table. They contained olives of various kinds, nuts and the usual salted cakes. She sat down opposite them.

Seymour had, of course, met her before but then it had been in the business part of the hotel, at reception. Now, in the soft darkness, she seemed completely different, her face more Arab, her eyes larger and darker, more Moroccan. She had partly uncovered her hair. In the hotel it had always been bound up in a kerchief. Now she had let it fall. It was dark and abundant and hung over her shoulders. Seymour sensed that this was significant. He knew that in Morocco a woman's hair was normally something to be strictly concealed. Was this a gesture of independence, an assertion of difference, a suggestion of other affiliations beside the Moroccan one? Looking at her now he could see how attractive she must have been once, how she could have drawn such men as de Lissac and Bossu. And also how strikingly her daughter resembled her.

There was a difference in the way they sat. The mother sat straight-backed, graceful but firm and unyielding. Chantale reclined rather than sat. It was again very graceful, very easy, very natural: but it was not the way any Englishwoman would have sat. Seymour knew he shouldn't be looking at her too much: but he was just about knocked out.

Initially Chantale's mother did not speak much, leaving the conversation to her daughter and Seymour, but gradually she let herself be drawn in.

He asked her how she liked running a hotel. She said that at first she had found it difficult because when her husband had died she had withdrawn into herself and then when they had moved into the hotel she had had to force herself out again. The public-ness of hotel life had shocked her and the constant need to assert herself. However, now she rather enjoyed it. It gave her a chance to meet people, different people from those she would usually have met, men especially, *hommes civilisés*, civilized men – a chance, she said, with a flash of her daughter's rebelliousness, that Moroccan women did not usually get!

Seymour said that he imagined that was particularly important for Chantale. Madame de Lissac agreed that it was and said that she was very grateful to those who had made it possible. And yet . . .

She hesitated.

And yet it was equally important that Chantale did not allow herself to be cut off from 'the other side' because that was her inheritance, too. That was what she had had in mind in bringing Chantale back here. She had grown up in the quarter and people remembered her from when she was a child. That made it easier for them to accept her. Even though, of course, she would always be different.

'You make me sound a freak,' said Chantale.

'Not a freak,' said Chantale's mother. 'Just different. And you will have to live with that.'

'I manage very well,' said Chantale.

'Yes, but what happens when you grow up?'

'Mother! I *am* grown up.'

'And need to find a husband?'

'Mother!' said Chantale, and got up hastily from the table, and took the bowls inside.

When her husband had died, she had said. Did she know how he had died, wondered Seymour? Did Chantale?

Seymour said that he could understand at least some of the difficulties, perhaps better than they might think. He told them about his own family: about the Polish grandfather who had served in the Tsarist army and been forced to leave Russia in a hurry because of his radical activities; about his grandfather on his mother's side, who had died in an Austro-Hungarian prison – also for unwise political activity; about the mother from Vojvodina, and the father who had grown up in England and wanted none of this sort of thing, only to be a boring, unrevolutionary Englishman –

'Were they all revolutionaries?' asked Chantale, who had returned with some bowls of hot, spicy soup.

'Yes. And I was the most revolutionary of the lot,' said Seymour. 'I joined the police.'

Madame de Lissac laughed.

'That I cannot understand,' said Chantale.

Seymour shrugged.

'In my part of London,' he said, 'which is a poor part, there weren't many jobs. I had tried an office and didn't like it. And the police gave me a chance to use my languages.'

'And they brought you to Tangier,' said Chantale, smiling.

'Can't be all bad, can it?' said Seymour.

They moved on to the main dish, which was couscous, made of semolina rolled into small, firm balls, steamed in saffron and spices, and served with a top layer of vegetables and meat.

Seymour asked Chantale's mother what it had been like when she was a child growing up in the area.

'It was very different then,' she said. 'That was under the old Sultan – not this one, but this one's father. In those days the Parasol meant something. My father worked for the Mahzen and that was something that gave prestige. It also made us quite well off. We were able to afford private tutors and so, although we were girls, we were quite well educated. We mixed, too, a little in society.

'But that had its dangers. We were seen, although we were always very discreet. I was seen, by a man, a Frenchman who did things for the Mahzen, and was very rich and ambitious. He wanted to marry me. I said no, and my father turned him down. But he pursued me. He just wouldn't give up. In the end they had to send me away to relatives in Algeria.

'Even there he pursued me. He just wouldn't give up. I think now that he couldn't bear to lose. Even when I told him that I had found someone else. I don't think he could believe that – believe it was possible, that anyone could be thought better than him. I tell you this,' she said, looking

Seymour directly in the face, 'so that you will understand. The man was Bossu.'

'I know already,' said Seymour.

She began to gather up the dishes. Chantale rose to help her but her mother signalled to her to sit down. She went off with the tray.

'She said, "When my husband died,"' said Seymour. 'Does she know how he died?'

'I think so,' said Chantale. 'We never speak of it but I think she has guessed.'

'And you: do you know how your father died?'

'Oh, yes,' said Chantale.

'Exactly how he died?'

Chantale looked at him.

'Exactly,' she said.

Chapter Fourteen

The first thing that Seymour noticed when he left the hotel the next morning was that Mustapha and Idris had changed their clothes. They were in bright new jellabas, Mustapha in a particularly splendid robe of saffron.

'What's this?' said Seymour.

'It's the end of Ramadan,' said Idris. 'Everyone puts on new clothes for the day.'

Seymour looked around. Yes, everyone was in new, or, at least, clean clothes; including Chantale, standing in the doorway beside him.

Seymour considered.

'Perhaps . . .?'

'Yes,' said Chantale, 'I think you should.'

He went back to his room and changed into his new suit, the one that Ali had made.

'Just a minute!' said Chantale and she stuck a large red handkerchief in his pocket.

'That makes you look more suitably festive,' she said.

He noticed that it matched the one draped round her shoulders.

'Yes,' she said, 'it shows that you belong to me.'

They went together to the Kasbah. The space in front of the Kasbah was taken up by lots of carpet-sided enclosures with seats inside them, in which people were sitting in their Sunday – or perhaps it was Friday, this being a Muslim country – best. Among them were the Macfarlanes.

'Come and sit beside me, Mr Seymour,' said Mrs Macfarlane.

Mustapha and Idris sat down on the other side of the carpet wall.

'You again!' said Macfarlane, with his habitual disfavour.

'A bodyguard!' said Mrs Macfarlane. 'How nice! I've always felt I should have one.'

She leaned over the carpet wall and chatted to Mustapha and Idris.

Chantale waved a hand and drifted off.

A procession began to pass in front of the enclosures. It consisted of splendidly fierce tribesmen on horseback, many of them sporting rows of medals, old men in white capes and often on donkeys, families in traditional draperies, well washed and much pressed, and French soldiers, who lined up at intervals along the front of the carpet boxes.

The Resident-General arrived, in a frock coat, top hat and high collar, and took up his position in one of the front boxes.

A small carriage appeared, drawn by four piebald ponies and escorted by French soldiers. Out of it climbed a little, much bewildered boy. He looked around, saw the Resident-General, and bowed to him. The Resident-General returned the bow. Then the little boy went into one of the boxes where a crowd of other small princes were sitting. He sat there stiffly for a moment or two and then, like them, turned round to have a good look at everyone.

Sheikh Musa appeared, bristling with medals and escorted by almost forty retainers, all on wonderful horses. He took up position to one side of the enclosures and looked balefully round.

There was a sudden stir at the Kasbah entrance and a lonely white figure rode out, sheltered by a great parasol. There was a murmur from the crowd.

'The Imperial Parasol,' whispered Mrs Macfarlane.

On foot and on either side of him walked venerable, bearded guards, gracefully wafting the flies away from the imperial face with sheets of white cloth. Behind them came the Imperial Guard – fifty huge Negroes in crimson uniforms, with black and white turbans, on pearl-grey horses.

And then – Seymour leaned forward. Everyone leaned forward.

'*Le voilà*,' said a man sitting on the other side of Macfarlane. 'There it is! *Le carosse de la Reine Victoria!*'

Yes, there it was, all red and gold and rickety, wheels grating on the dusty street, empty, pulled by slaves and escorted by guards: the state chariot presented to the Sultan of a previous day by Queen Victoria.

The frail figure beneath the parasol passed in front of them. Caids and pashas, and then the crowd, bent low. The Europeans inclined their heads. Seymour caught a glimpse of a thin, drawn face. And then the figure passed out of sight and Musa and his men wheeled in behind him.

'Will they keep it up?' asked Mrs Macfarlane. 'Next year?'

'Probably,' said Macfarlane. 'Only it won't be him next year. He's abdicating this afternoon.'

After the Royal Ceremony to mark the end of Ramadan, the crowd, now in festive spirit, moved on to the pig-sticking. It was the last one in the series and that on its own was enough to guarantee a splendid turn-out. The space all round the Tent was jammed with people in their finery and there seemed more riders than ever in the enclosure.

Musa's chief outrider, Ahmet, was about to set off to run the pigs but Seymour managed to catch him in time to get him to identify the two men who had ridden outrider on the other side of the hunt on the day that Bossu had been killed, Ibrahim and Riyad. They could remember the occasion very well and recalled the rider coming up late, and,

214

no, it certainly wasn't a woman, it was a . . . And they could recall the horse exactly.

In no time at all the bugle sounded and the riders climbed on to their horses and prepared to move off.

'Come on!' said Idris impatiently.

'I'm okay here.'

'No, no, if we don't get started, we'll miss –'

'That's okay.'

Mustapha and Idris stared at him.

'You mean –?'

'I'm not going this time.'

'But, but –'

'I've seen what I wanted.'

'You mean you're not going to follow the hunt?'

'That's right.'

'But –'

'You can if you want to.'

'But –'

'It will be all right. Ali Khadr is going to the mosque. So Chantale's mother tells me.'

Mustapha and Idris conferred.

'We'll just go part of the way.'

'That's all right.'

At the last moment Mustapha pulled out.

'It's a question of honour,' he muttered.

'I won't go far,' said Idris, weakening by the minute.

He returned after a very short time.

'It's a question of honour,' he said, depressed.

The riders disappeared in a cloud of dust. Beyond them some figures quietly browsing in the scrub looked up, startled, and then began to run for their lives.

The crowd shot off; but very soon people began to fall out. The horses, too, soon began to feel the pace and some of them dropped behind.

The many who had come out of the Tent to watch the start began to file back in. At one end of the long bar Seymour saw Juliette talking to a young officer with his arm in a sling, consoling him, no doubt, for being unable to take part in the chase.

Someone touched his arm. It was Monique.

'Here again,' she said, 'as you see. Just can't stop.'

'Forget about him,' said Seymour. 'He wasn't worth it.'

'I know.'

'Find someone else,' said Seymour. 'He did.'

'I'll keep trying,' promised Monique, and slipped away.

Seymour could see Chantale on the other side of the Tent, working her way around groups of people as usual, getting material for her column, no doubt. But he didn't go over to her.

Mrs Macfarlane appeared beside him.

'You're leaving us, I gather?'

'I'm afraid so.'

'I shall be sorry to see you go.'

'And I to leave.'

She followed his eyes.

'You know,' she said, 'it is going to be very difficult for Chantale.'

'I know,' he said.

'And will become even more difficult,' she said, 'as time goes by. Unless she marries a Frenchman. She is too old, in Moroccan terms, to marry a Moroccan. And would she be content with the kind of life that would mean?'

'She should marry a Frenchman,' said Seymour.

'She might not want to,' said Mrs Macfarlane, and moved away.

The huntsmen were beginning to return. Sheikh Musa appeared in the door of the Tent. He saw Seymour and came across to him.

216

'You've heard about the abdication?'

'Yes.'

'You know who's going to be the next Sultan?'

'Moulay Hafiz?'

'That's right.'

He smiled and took Seymour's arm.

'Advise me,' he said. 'Would it be a good idea to invite Moulay to the next pig-sticking?'

'Would it be worth it?' said Seymour. 'They'd only get another one.'

Seymour went out into the enclosure.

Monsieur Ricard was being helped off his horse.

'And this,' hissed his daughter, 'is the last time for you!'

'I fell off,' said Ricard, depressed.

'He tried to get on again,' said Millet. 'But the horse wasn't having any.'

'At least the horse had some sense,' said Suzanne.

The soldiers were coming in, lances bloodied.

'You did pretty well today, Levret,' one of them was saying.

'I only got one,' Levret said.

'They weren't easy today.'

'I could have done better.'

De Grassac went past, leading his horse.

'A good ride?' asked Seymour.

'A good ride,' said de Grassac. 'But no stick.'

'Could I have a word with you?'

De Grassac handed the reins to a trooper.

'At your service.'

Seymour took him aside.

'I suppose it's the army,' he said, 'that teaches you to think quickly in an emergency.'

'Well, yes, it does. But –'

'Such as when you couldn't get the lance free again. You had stuck too well.'

217

'What are you saying?'

'After you had stuck Bossu. A good stick, a very good stick. But then you couldn't get the lance out again. It had stuck in the earth. So there you were, with someone coming up, and the lance in your hand, and the point in Bossu's back. Quick thinking required. And this is probably where the army helped you.'

'What the hell are you talking about?'

'You left Bossu, with your lance still sticking in him, picked up his lance and rode off.'

'Monsieur Seymour –'

'And rejoined the hunt. Late, of course. You had to ride like the wind. That was what one observer said. With your headdress trailing out behind, like hair. But you came up in time to be in at the killing. And, of course, you had a lance. Bossu's lance.'

This time de Grassac said nothing.

'When the news came in about Bossu, you went back and recovered your own lance. Quite openly. And then when I asked you for the lance that had killed Bossu, you could give one to me. Bossu's own. Incidentally, I took it to the shop you told me of. You were right, they couldn't tell me who it belonged to. But it had been mended once and they thought the work might have been done for a Monsieur Bossu.

'It was the lance,' Seymour explained, 'that had originally set me thinking. Because there was somebody else's lance, still stuck in Bossu. But where was his own lance?'

'Stolen,' said de Grassac.

'I remember you making much of the way things were stolen out here. But I spoke to someone who was on the scene immediately afterwards, *immediately* afterwards, and they couldn't remember seeing another lance, lying by the body, say. It was one of the things that puzzled me. I thought that perhaps the killer had taken it. But why? Perhaps so that he could rejoin the hunt without anyone suspecting. He would need a lance, wouldn't he?

218

'There was some evidence that whoever had killed Bossu had ridden off in that direction. And further evidence, later, that whoever it was had been wearing a headdress – it got caught in the thorns. But my informant supposed that it belonged perhaps to one of Sheikh Musa's men. I was able to check with Sheikh Musa's men. In particular, with the two men who had been outriding on the south side. Of course, they didn't see what happened when you rode in after Bossu. But they did see someone riding up hard afterwards and overtaking the field. They were able to tell me who it was. Going not so much by the person as by the horse. They are pretty good at recognizing horses. They described it to me, and I have just confirmed that the description matches yours. But, of course, we don't need my identification. Theirs will do. But I can get them to confirm it, if necessary.'

'Don't bother,' said Captain de Grassac.

'I think I know why you killed him, too. When de Lissac was blown up in the truck, Chantale asked you to go down south and look into it. Because I think that even then she suspected that it was not an accident. You went down and looked into it. And then you told her that it was, indeed, an accident. Yes?'

'Yes.'

'Why?'

'Better for her not to know. I knew, and that was enough.'

'Could I ask how you knew? I know, too, but that is because I have talked to eyewitnesses. But I don't think you can have talked to them.'

'No. It was the dancers, the Chleuh dancers. They circulate all over the south. They pick up things. And they picked up this. And then they talked to me.'

'Why didn't you report it? Tell the authorities?'

'What authorities?'

'Well –'

'There aren't any down there. There is only Moulay Hafiz. And the army. But what is the point of telling the army? Bossu wasn't under its jurisdiction. And nor, by this time, was de Lissac.'

'You thought you knew what to do?'

'I *did* know what to do.'

A little to de Grassac's surprise, Seymour left him and walked back into the Tent. There he found Chantale.

'I have been expecting this,' said Chantale.

'Since when?'

'Since I saw you talking to Armand de Grassac.'

'Not before?'

'Well, perhaps since you spoke to me last night.'

'You knew that your father had been murdered.'

'Yes.'

'How? Did de Grassac tell you.'

'No. Not directly. But I read him like an open book. He is a straightforward honest man, and hopeless at deceiving. However, I had worked it out before. I knew that Bossu had put my father up to the journey with the explosives. And I don't think for one moment that he had done it out of the goodness of his heart. My father did. He was another like Armand de Grassac. Unable to believe that anyone could be so evil. But I knew. And when Armand came back, that confirmed it.'

'So what did you do?'

'Looked for revenge. Or justice, as I would prefer to call it.'

'How?'

'Through my writing. The article I planted in *New Dawn* was just the beginning. I thought that in the end I would get him through my writing. It would be slow, but that,' she said, looking Seymour straight in the face, 'would only make it sweeter.'

'You didn't go further?'

220

'I would have, probably. Only Armand got there before me.'

'Did you know what he was going to do? Did you talk about it? He, of course, won't tell me. But perhaps you will.'

'No, we didn't talk. And no, I didn't know. But if I had, I would have been with him all the way. I tell you this because I don't want you to think Armand was alone. If he is to blame, so am I.'

She laid her hand on his arm.

'You know, I think, what you mean to me. And I, I think, mean something to you. If that is so, can I take advantage of it to ask a favour? See that Armand is not treated too harshly.'

In the end he decided to consult Mrs Macfarlane.

'Hmm.'

She thought for a moment.

'This is, actually, as my husband would say, a ticklish legal problem. Under whose jurisdiction might this fall? This happened in Tangier. Tangier's legal status is as yet undefined. An international zone? Maybe, but tomorrow. Today? Morocco? France? And in practice?' She thought some more.

'You know,' she said, 'I believe justice might best be served by going to Monsieur Lambert. The one thing certain in all this is that de Grassac is under military law. I don't think that anyone is going to complain too much if this is left to the army to sort out.

'Not the international powers, certainly, who won't want to get involved. Nor the government in France, and not the settlers here, who would do well to keep quiet about Bossu. The Mahzen? Not just at the moment, with Moulay Hafiz taking over.

'No, leave the army to sort out its own dirty washing. And for once, I suspect, they will sort it out very sensibly. You know, there is a custom in Morocco known as "God's door". You should always leave the door open. Being too cut-and-dried on anything is a mistake. I suspect the army in Morocco is well aware of this custom and if ever there was a case for its application, this is it.'

Mr Bahnini came to see him.

'To say goodbye,' he said.

'You're leaving?'

'I'm going back to Casablanca. To set up as a book-keeper. I think that when the Protectorate is established, there will be a lot of demand for my services.'

'I think you could be right.'

They shook hands.

'Macfarlane will miss you.'

'Less than you might think. Sadiq will be replacing me.'

'Really?'

Sadiq looked rather shame-faced.

'He talked me into it,' he said. 'Macfarlane. He said that if I wished to stop the French from taking everything over, the way to do it was to get Tangier made into a free international zone: and that the best way for me to do that was to come and work for the committee.'

And Awad? Awad was going into politics.

'Of which,' said Mr Bahnini, 'there is likely to be a lot in future.'

Mustapha and Idris embraced him and wept.

'We've sort of got used to you,' they said. 'In fact, this doesn't seem a bad line of business at all.'

Seymour left recommendations all over the place. However, he placed greater reliance on Chantale's mother, who had promised to keep an eye on them.

On Chantale Seymour thought long and deep.

'She will always be torn,' he said to Madame de Lissac, 'between the French side and the Moroccan side of her. The only way out that I can see is to add a moderating influence. Let's call it the English side, and I will do my best to see that she remains as true to that as to the others.'